BLOOD RUNS DEEP

STEPHEN TAYLOR

STEPHEN TAYLOR BOOKS

COVER DESIGN BY
DISSECT DESIGNS
WWW.DISSECTDESIGNS.COM

Copyright © 2021 Stephen Taylor
All rights reserved.
ISBN: 978-1-7391636-5-5

DANNY PEARSON WILL RETURN

For updates about current and upcoming releases, as well as exclusive promotions, visit the authors website at:

www.stephentaylorbooks.com

ALSO BY STEPHEN TAYLOR
THE DANNY PEARSON THRILLER SERIES

Snipe

Heavy Traffic

The Timekeepers Box

The Book Signing

Vodka Over London Ice

Execution Of Faith

Who Holds The Power

Alive Until I Die

Sport of Kings

Blood Runs Deep

Command To Kill

No Upper Limit

Leave Nothing To Chance

CHAPTER 1

Looking at his watch, then up at the grand, mid-19th century facade of the Gare du Nord Paris Metro, Danny Pearson continued to look for his target while polishing off the rest of his Whopper burger. He glanced at the man's picture on his phone, then sat back under Burger King's outside canopy, and resumed his watchful eye.

Five minutes later, his target, Miles Marshbrook, emerged from the train station. The tall, skinny, nervous man with a leather overnight bag slung across his shoulder looked both ways before scurrying across the road. He walked past Danny and disappeared out of sight, heading off down the Boulevard de Strasbourg.

Danny drained the rest of his drink through the straw. He was in no hurry to follow; he knew where Marshbrook was heading. What did interest him were the two Middle Eastern men who exited the train station a minute later. They took a quick glance either way before crossing the road, their eyes locking back onto Marshbrook as they followed him down the Boulevard de Strasbourg.

Danny slid the food wrappers into the bin and strolled out of the canopied shade into the hot summer sun. With the boulevard full of Parisians and tourists, Danny knew Marshbrook would be relatively safe until he checked into his reservation at the Hotel Relais Du Louvre, opposite the famous Louvre art museum next to the river Seine. His brief from Howard was simple: meet Miles Marshbrook in room 18 of the hotel, exchange money for the information Mr Marshbrook claims to have regarding the identity of an inside man who has been selling Ministry of Defence weapon designs to the Middle East.

Not wanting to turn up late to the party, and due to the location of the meet, Danny had taken an educated guess that Marshbrook would take the train into the city. Following at the rear of the procession, Danny studied the look and movement of the two Middle Eastern men ahead of him. They were wearing zipped-up jackets even though it was swelteringly hot, suggesting concealed weapons, and they walked with purpose: upright, regimented, military trained with rock-steady, focused heads on solid necks. Danny's best guess was Saudi secret services.

They crossed onto Boulevard de Sebastopol and continued down towards the river, the two men ahead peeling off and entering a shop while Marshbrook walked into Starbucks to get a coffee. Danny continued to walk along the tree-lined boulevard, passing all three of them to cross the road and turn down towards the Pont au Change bridge. Picking up his pace, he followed the river towards the Louvre. Within five minutes, Danny was sitting on a bench across from a grand Gothic church, and in sight of the entrance to the Hotel Relais Du Louvre.

It didn't take long for Marshbrook to approach the hotel from the more direct route. He looked around nervously before entering, obvious to the trained eye that he didn't know what he was supposed to be looking for. The two Middle Eastern men entered the hotel a minute later, still visible to Danny through the front window as they pretended to look at the tourist board inside the foyer while Marshbrook checked in. Moving closer, Danny tucked in behind an Enterprise rental van parked opposite the hotel. Peeping around the back of it, he could see Marshbrook taking the room keys from the receptionist and heading away to the stairs at the rear of the hotel. Once Marshbrook was out of sight, the pretty, dark-haired receptionist turned her attention to the two Middle Eastern men, a smile on her face as she asked them if she could help. To Danny's surprise, one of the men pulled a silenced handgun from his jacket and shot the young woman in the forehead, the shocked look locked on her face as she toppled off the back of the reception chair. Without delay, the other man moved around the back of the reception desk and pushed the woman out of sight in the space under it. Danny crossed the road, his eyes locked on the two men as they headed out of sight up the stairs.

Shit, that went sour quickly.

Moving inside, Danny pulled his own silenced Glock from his jacket and headed to the stairs. The stairwell was old and small in the centuries-old building, giving no view up the centre from the bottom to top. Taking the steps as fast as he could go without making a sound, Danny moved up each floor, stopping to listen on the landing, and continuing up when he couldn't hear anyone. When he finally reached the top floor, he darted his head into the landing, taking a quick mental snapshot of the empty corridor before entering and heading towards room 18. As he got closer, he could see the door slightly ajar. Standing to one side, Danny moved his ear close to the gap and listened. He could hear voices, too faint to tell what they were saying, but he guessed they would be facing away from the door as they questioned Marshbrook. With his gun raised, Danny took a few deep breaths, tensing and relaxing his leg muscles, priming them for fast movement as he played out a surprise shock-and-awe attack in his mind.

One, two, three.

Danny burst through the door with astounding speed, his gun up and ready to shoot both men as they turned. His plans were scuppered when he saw them facing him with their guns pointing in his direction. On his second step into the room, Danny planted his right leg on the wall beside him and kicked himself sideways through the en-suite door as a bullet whizzed past his ear, punching a neat hole through the hotel door behind him.

'Stop, we need him alive,' shouted one of the men to the other.

In the en-suite, Danny flipped himself into the large cast iron bath. Firing over the lip, he punched a neat line of holes in the direction of the Middle Eastern men through the tile, wood and plaster wall that separated the en-suite from the bedroom. He heard grunts of pain as he found his target, followed by a stream of bullets erupting back his way, showering him in bits of plaster and tiles before striking the side of the heavy cast iron bathtub with a deafening clang.

When the gunfire ceased, Danny could just about hear heavy breathing and grunts of pain above the ringing in his ears. Poking his head above the tub, he closed one eye and looked through a bullet hole into the bedroom. He could see one man face down on the bed, and the legs of someone on the floor. Climbing out of the tub, Danny spun out of the en-suite into the bedroom, his gun trained on the man sitting on the floor, his back propped up against the outside wall. He looked at Danny with defeated eyes, blood oozing from his chest. The gun was still in his hand, but he no longer had the strength to lift it.

Danny turned to Marshbrook sitting in the corner, a crimson flood covering his white shirt from his freshly opened-up neck. Flipping open Marshbrook's overnight bag, Danny found a Manila folder. He opened it to find details of the hotel booking and details of a job interview for an IT company in Paris. The name on the booking and interview was Jean Paul Marcellas. There was no information, no exchange. He'd been set up.

Danny folded the papers up and put them in his pocket before rifling through the pockets of the dead man on the bed. He went through the wallet. No ID, no cards, just some cash. Crouching down in front of the man sitting against the wall, Danny slapped him lightly on the cheek.

'Who do you work for?' he said.

The man looked at him with semi-conscious eyes. His mouth was moving, but no sound was coming out. Without expression, Danny reached over, grabbed a pillow off the bed and shoved it over the man's face. He pushed the silencer of his gun into the middle of the pillow and pulled the trigger with a dull metallic ping. The man's body jerked before slumping back down. Throwing the pillow to one side, Danny removed the man's phone and some vehicle keys. He placed the man's thumb on the phone to unlock it and frowned when his own picture looked back at him. Pocketing the phone, Danny picked up the vehicle keys and stood. He noticed the Enterprise keyring on the keys and walked to the window. With a press of the button, Danny watched the hazard lights of the van below flash as it unlocked.

Feeling the need to get out, Danny took a neatly folded towel off the chair and went into the bathroom. He wiped down the cast iron bath and doors on the way out, taking the towel with him to avoid leaving any DNA. A minute later he was out of the hotel. He looked up and down the narrow road as he crossed to the Enterprise rental van. All was quiet, just the odd Parisian and tourist. Danny got into the van and started it up. He glanced in the back before pulling away, frowning at the sight of a crate with its lid off. The inside was lined with foam, handcuffs and chains were fixed to its thick wooden sides. With the unnerving thought that someone wanted him kidnapped and crated, Danny pulled into the Paris traffic.

CHAPTER 2

'Wait here,' she said, leaving her bodyguards in the foyer of The Savoy Hotel without waiting for an answer.

'Good evening, Miss Volkov,' said the ma"tre d' of Kaspar's restaurant.

'Good evening, Samuel. You have my usual table ready?' she said, her voice polite but cold and unemotional, with a heavy Russian accent.

'Of course, and your guest is already here,' said Samuel, walking ahead of her to get her seated.

The heels of her Christian Louboutins tapped rhythmically as she followed. Heads turned as she passed through the restaurant in a figure-hugging designer dress, that complimented her long blonde hair and striking, ice-blue eyes.

James Bullman got up out of his seat to greet her as she approached. 'Annika, my dear, so good to see you,' he said, sitting back down as Samuel slid the chair in behind Annika as she sat.

'Can I get you something to drink?' said Samuel, handing them menus.

'Beluga vodka on the rocks,' said Annika, her eyes fixed on James.

'Eh, just tonic water for me, please. I've got cabinet meetings this afternoon,' James said, his political face locked in its usual public smile.

As Samuel left, James looked back to Annika, her unwavering, ice-cold stare causing his smile to falter for a second before he composed himself.

'He got away,' she said in a blunt statement of fact.

'Er, yes, I'm afraid he did.'

'What kind of imbeciles did you send?' said Annika, leaning in as she spoke angrily.

'They were highly trained assets. Look, I did as you asked. It's not my fault Pearson got away. Now, this is not the time or place to discuss it,' he said, his voice hushed and eyes flicking around nervously in case they were overheard.

'Do not dare to silence me, Mr Bullman. I may be young, but I am my father's daughter. He owned you. Now I own you,' said Annika, her voice returning to its calm and chilling tone.

'Now listen here, young lady. Whatever agreement your father and I had, it ended when he died. I arranged Paris out of respect for him, but that's it. No more,' said James, his face reddening at being spoken to by this young upstart.

'You know, Mr Bullman, when the trustees released my father's business affairs to me on my twenty-first birthday, I spent much time going through his journals and business effects.' Annika paused, her face expressionless as she stared unblinkingly at Bullman. His practiced political facade hid his thoughts, but his eyes gave away his growing nerves.

'There is some very interesting video footage in there, some that would cause even the most broad-minded members of your constituency to be shocked by your sexual preferences. A taste so niche I believe one of the women from the brothel ended up in hospital and still carries the scars,' said Annika, pausing once again to watch the colour drain from Bullman's face.

'I did not spend five years trying to find out who killed my father, to give up, Mr Bullman. The arrangements are made. All you have to do is deliver him. Daniel Pearson will suffer, and when I decide the time is right, he will beg me to kill him. Get it done, Mr Bullman. Do I make myself clear?'

'Perfectly. Now if you'll excuse me, I've rather lost my appetite,' said James, getting up to leave.

Samuel arrived with the drink as Bullman left. 'Is your guest not staying?' he asked.

'I'm afraid Mr Bullman had some pressing business to deal with, so I will be dining alone tonight,' Annika said, taking a sip of her Beluga vodka on the rocks.

'Very good, madam,' said Samuel, giving Annika a menu before clearing Mr Bullman's cutlery and glass away.

CHAPTER 3

Reluctant to use his Eurostar train ticket in case whoever planned the ambush knew how he travelled to Paris, Danny drove the rental van the three and a half hours to Calais. Driving around the outskirts of town, Danny pulled the van to a halt just short of a refugee camp. He wiped the steering wheel and door free of any fingerprints, noting a group of travel- and life-weary refugees watching him from the roadside. Leaving the driver's door open and the keys in the ignition, Danny got out and walked off towards the ferry port. He doubted the van would be there for long. Stopping in the middle of town, Danny bought a pay as you go mobile and called his best friend, Scott Miller. His own phone and the one he'd taken off the Middle Eastern man had been turned off since Paris in case they were being tracked.

'Hello,' said Scott reservedly at the unknown number.

'Scott, it's Danny. I need your help, mate.'

'Mmm, that sounds ominous. What do you need, old chap?' said Scott, his curiosity piqued.

'Can you pick me up from Dover ferry terminal around eight o'clock?'

'No problem, but you'll owe me one. I'll have to cancel my dinner date with a rather dishy brunette,' said Scott with a little chuckle in his voice.

'Thanks Scott, I appreciate it, and Scott, don't tell anyone you've spoken to me,' said Danny, noticing the ferry terminal in the distance.

'Mum's the word. I'll see you later.'

Danny hung up and carried on walking. He couldn't help smiling at Scott. His friend loved a bit of cloak-and-dagger, but could always be relied on to help.

After buying a ticket as a walk-on passenger, Danny boarded the P&O ferry and made for the restaurant. He ploughed through overcooked fish and dry chips, contemplating who would want him dead, and more importantly, who would want him kidnapped and why. The who-would-want-him-dead list was quick, easy and fairly long; the who-would-want-him-kidnapped left him puzzled and frustrated. When he'd finished eating, Danny went up on deck and stared at the pay as you go mobile for a while before making a call.

'Oxford Financial Consultants, how may I help you?' said an upbeat woman.

'I need to speak to Howard,' said Danny to the contact front for the government agent who had sent Danny to Paris.

'Who's speaking please?' came the polite response.

'Roger Freeman,' said Danny, using an old alias.

'Stay on this number, Mr Freeman, you will be contacted shortly.'

The phone line went dead the instant she had stopped talking. It rang again within a minute with no caller ID.

'Howard.'

'Good evening, Daniel. Glad you're still with us. We were starting to worry. Do share, dear boy; enquiring minds are rather anxious to know why there's a receptionist and three dead men in a hotel in Paris,' said Howard, in his usual upbeat manner.

'The whole thing was a setup, a kidnap plan. There was no Marshbrook, just some poor French guy who thought he was going for a job interview. The two Middle Eastern guys had my photo on their phone. They had a hire van outside the hotel with a crate and chains to transport me somewhere,' said Danny, not disguising his anger.

'I see. That does raise some concerns. Are you injured?'

'No, I'm fine. Where did the information for the contract come from, Howard?' said Danny, his mind still turning over what happened.

'One of our own. I need time to look into this. Keep off-grid and I'll call you as soon as I have some answers. I assume no one else knows this number?' said Howard, an unusual hint of concern in his voice.

'No,' was all Danny said in response.

'Good, I'll talk to you soon,' said Howard, ending the call.

Putting the phone in his pocket, Danny watched Dover grow in the distance as the sun set over the Channel behind him. He glanced at his trusty G-Shock watch. He still had an hour until his pick-up from Scott.

CHAPTER 4

Back in his office in the MoD building in Whitehall, James Bullman sat back in his large leather chair, drumming his fingers on the walnut, inlaid leather desk. Deep creases etched into his forehead as he brooded over his predicament.

When the Volkov Russian Mafia family had been run out of London, and later killed at their family estate in Moscow after a turf war between them and London gangster, Harry Knight, he'd thought his troubles were over. He thought the blackmail over his stupid indiscretions at the Volkovs brothel, and the threats and intimidation were history. And they had been. For five years, nothing. He'd risen through the ranks to Minister of Defence and revelled in the power and freedom it had given him. That was until Annika Volkov breezed into London to bring it all back, her icy blue eyes and cold, unreadable demeanour identical to her father's, as was her business manner. Now he was stuck. His only chance to redeem the situation was to bargain this man Pearson for the video footage she had against him. Damn those idiots in Paris. If they'd just done their job right, he'd be free of Annika Volkov. His mobile rang and tore him away from his thoughts.

'Yes.'

'Sorry to bother you so late, sir, it's Larry Whistle. You told me to phone you if we had anything on the target.'

'Yes, Larry, what is it?' said James, sitting up in anticipation.

'Daniel Pearson's passport flagged at Calais ferry terminal earlier this evening. We hacked the Dover ferry port camera feeds and got a visual on him as he entered the UK. He got into a white Porsche registered to a Scott Miller. We've been tracking it with traffic cams and it's heading for central London. Would you like us to intercept, sir?'

'No, just track him for me please. He's only flagged as a person of interest at the moment. Just let me know what his final destination is,' said James, the creases in his forehead relaxing as the bargaining chip moved closer to his grasp.

'Yes sir. Good night sir.'

'Good night, Larry, and thank you,' said James, hanging up.

He sat back in his chair, his fingers resuming their drumming on the table as he pondered his next move. After a few seconds he reached forward, picked up his mobile and selected a contact. It rang for quite a while, only being picked up as James was about to give up.

'James, what's so important to be calling at this time?' came a sleepy voice.

'Sorry, Terence, can't be helped. I have a situation that requires your assistance. I'm afraid I'm going to have to call in that favour you owe me,' said James, his words apologetic, but the tone in his voice was telling, not asking.

'Go on,' said Chief Superintendent Terence Crawford,

bluntly.

'I'm going to need one of your armed response units to arrest someone for me.'

'And the paperwork for the arrest?' said Terence with a sinking feeling in his stomach as he anticipated the answer.

'Strictly off the books. I'll need him delivered to a specific location,' James said with the calm confidence of a man in power.

'I'm sorry, James, I can't just authorise an operation like this with no paperwork. I'm the Chief Superintendent for Christ's sake. If it came out, it would finish me,' said Terence raising his voice, annoyed.

'I think you forget how you got to be Chief Superintendent in the first place. You're welcome by the way,' said James, returning the tone of voice.

An uneasy silence followed. The only sound was the ticking of an old clock in James's office, adding tension to the pause.

'When?' Terence finally said.

'Tomorrow morning, I'll text you the details later,' said James, a smile curling up on his face as he enjoyed the power he had over Terence Crawford.

As Terence hung up, disgruntled. James knew he had to do his bidding. He'd accelerated Terence's career to Chief Superintendent and could just as easily take it all away from him, and that was something he would do if he had to. His confidence rising, James was suitably revved up enough to deal with Annika Volkov. He grabbed the phone once more and hit the call button.

'Yes,' said Annika, cold and blunt.

'I have some news on Pearson,' he said with an air of arrogance.

'Tell me,' Annika said, demanding a response.

'I can deliver him to you tomorrow.'

'Very good, Mr Bullman, I'm impressed,' she said, her voice still in monotone coldness.

'There is a condition. I want the video footage and anything else you have on me. I deliver Pearson to you and our relationship ends. Do I make myself clear?' said James, his confidence and arrogance fully restored.

It waned a little as the phone fell silent for the second time that night. The seconds ticked away and James could feel a cold sweat of uncertainty washing over him.

'Very well, deliver Pearson and I will give you what you want,' she finally said.

'Good, have your men ready. It will happen tomorrow. I'll call with the where and when,' said James hanging up and breathing a sigh of relief.

Standing, James flicked his jacket off the back of the chair, he put it on and headed out the door, clicking the lights off as he went. He passed one of the night cleaners in their blue overalls and peaked baseball cap. His head was down as he polished the corridor floor with a circular buffing machine. James walked on, heading down the stairs without acknowledging or giving a second thought to the cleaner. The man continued buffing the floor until he reached the door to James's office. Turning the machine off, he glanced both ways and slipped inside. Without turning the light on, he worked by the orange glow of London's street lamps coming in through the window. He stuck a tiny listening device on the underside of the office chair, another one just out of sight on the back of the filing cabinet, and a final one underneath the old walnut office desk.

'Sound test, one two, one two.'

His mobile buzzed with the emoji of a thumbs up, and he exited the room. He was back buffing the floor less than sixty seconds after entering the office.

CHAPTER 5

Not too far away from the MoD building in Whitehall was another government owned building. The purpose of this building was only known to a select few. The government man known only as Howard walked into the office. Four night shift analysts sat glued to their computer screens as he moved amongst them.

'Any news for me, Brian?'

'Yes sir. Mr Bullman just made two calls. One to Police Chief Superintendent Terence Crawford and the other to an unregistered mobile in Westminster. He wasn't on long enough to get an exact location.'

'Very good, thank you, Brian,' said Howard, turning to a scruffy techie guy with an unkempt beard and a beanie hat on his dark, greasy hair. 'How's our man getting on with the bugs, Martin?'

'All in place, sir.'

'Good, very good. I'll leave you gentlemen to it. Let me know of any developments,' said Howard, turning to leave.

'Sir?' said another analyst, stopping Howard mid-step.

'Yes William.'

'Is this strictly legal? I mean, he is the Minister of Defence,' said a nervous William.

'That's a good question, William, and you're right to ask it, but don't worry, I have the authority to investigate anyone who may pose a threat to the welfare of this country. The only people I answer to are the Prime Minister and the Queen. As for Minister of Defence James Bullman, the Paris job was sanctioned from information apparently provided by one of Minister Bullman's sources, and anyone who lays a trap for one of my assets gets my full and undivided attention. Good night, William,' Howard said, his tone jovial as always.

'Good night, sir,' replied William, his mind put at ease.

Howard took the lift down to the underground parking bays and climbed into the back of a waiting Audi Q7.

'Where to, sir?' said the driver.

'Home please, Frank. I won't need you again until the morning,' said Howard with a smile to the eyes looking at him in the rear-view mirror.

'Very good, sir,' said Frank, moving forward as the large metal gate slid aside, allowing him to drive up the access ramp to the road outside.

As the large, quiet car moved through the late evening London traffic, Howard pondered on the events of the last couple of days. He and Danny had somewhat of a love-hate relationship, but he was still the best asset he'd ever had, and the thought, let alone the reason, that someone wanted to kidnap him unsettled Howard greatly. Tomorrow he would push Bullman about his source for the Paris job and get Danny to a safe house until he had some answers.

'Tough day, sir?' said Frank, noting Howard's tense look in the mirror.

'Yes, Frank, most of them seem to be these days. Anyway, how are you? The wife and kids all well?' said Howard, a kind smile crossing his face as he asked.

'They're all good, thank you, sir. Would you believe my Sophie's turning twenty-eight at the weekend? I don't know where the time goes,' said Frank, a grin of pride on his face.

'That's great, Frank, send them all my best,' said Howard, suddenly lost in thought.

'Thank you, sir, I will do,' said Frank, pulling up outside Howard's house.

As Howard left him and entered his empty home, he wished he had a family like Frank's, but he was married to the job, and in his kind of job, there was no place for a wife and kids.

CHAPTER 6

With the events in Paris preying heavily on his mind, Danny woke to the first rays of the sun through Scott's guest room curtains. He rolled over and grabbed his trusty but battered G-Shock watch, checking the time and groaning at the 5:30am staring back at him. Getting up, Danny padded across the hall in his pants and T-shirt and went into Scott's fourth bedroom-cum-small gym. He found a pair of Scott's shorts and put them on before grabbing his trainers. He left a note for Scott in the kitchen and borrowed the entry fob to get back into the apartment block.

Ignoring the confines of the lift, Danny took the stairs and exited the modern metal and glass tower block, with its multi-million-pound apartments overlooking the Thames and skyscrapers of the Isle of Dogs opposite. The early morning air was fresh, but as the summer sun rose above the horizon and cut its way between the buildings, its rays warmed his face. Danny broke into a slow jog, increasing the pace as his muscles loosened up until he was running at full pelt. When his heart and lungs couldn't keep up with the demand any longer, he slowed to a walk, sucking in great gulps of air until he'd recovered. Leaning against the metal railings of the riverside path, Danny stretched and took in the London skyline before turning and jogging back towards Scott's.

––––––

Rubbing the sleep out of his eyes, Scott plodded into the kitchen.

'Daniel, old man, I can hear your phone ringing,' he said out loud, spotting the note saying he'd gone for a run just as he finished speaking.

'I guess I'd better answer it then,' muttered Scott, as he went into his spare bedroom and picked up Danny's pay as you go phone off the side.

'Hello.'

There was a moment's silence on the other end. 'Scott, is that you?'

'Eh, yes, who might this be?' said Scott, puzzled.

'It's Howard. Where's Danny?'

'Howard, lovely to hear from you. He's out running. Hang on, I'll see if I can see him,' said Scott moving to the lounge and pressing the remote for the electric blinds to open.

––––––

Scott's building came into view as Danny ran past an identical block of riverfront apartments next door. His senses were immediately put on alert by a navy Transit van parked on double yellow lines near the entrance. Shooting his head right he caught a glimpse of a man in a baseball cap talking into a radio as he tucked behind the corner of a building out of sight. With the events of Paris still fresh in his mind, Danny turned on his heels and prepared to take flight back down the path that followed the river front. A police riot van screamed down the road in front of him, cutting him off. Members of a police tactical team burst out of the navy Transit and appeared from behind the buildings, cutting him off front and back.

'Armed police! Down on your knees, hands on your head, NOW!' bellowed the lead officer.

With barrels of the unit's MP5 submachine guns pointing at his head, Danny slowly dropped to his knees and placed his hands on his head. He stared at them, defiance burning in his eyes as they pushed him flat on his front, his hands pulled roughly behind him as they cuffed him. Scooping him up under the armpits, they bundled him into the caged section in the back of the riot van.

———

'Oh my gosh, Howard, they've got him, er, the police. Sorry, a bunch of armed police just pounced on Daniel outside my apartment. They're driving away now,' said Scott in flap as he stared out of his lounge window at the scene below.

'You're sure they're police?' said Howard, calm as always.

'Yes, it's written on their jackets, and they put him in a police van.'

'Ok, Scott, what's the number on the top of the police van?'

'Er, hang on. The roof of the van has 52, with CP20 written behind it.'

'Good, thank you, Scott. I'll take it from here,' said Howard before the line went dead.

'Eh, right. I suppose that's it then,' said Scott to himself, and he watched the police vehicles disappear out of sight.

CHAPTER 7

nitially Danny hadn't been worried about being arrested; a call to his friend and Chief of the Secret Intelligence Service, Edward Jenkins, or the high-level government man and his handler, Howard, and they would have him out of nick in a flash. His concerns grew the minute they put him in the van without charging him or reading him his rights.

'Oi, what am I charged with?' Danny shouted to the back of the officer driving the riot van in convoy through the London traffic, with a squad car in front and the navy Transit van behind.

The man blanked him completely. Another ten minutes passed uncomfortably as Danny bounced up and down on the hard plastic seat, unable to steady himself around the corners with his hands cuffed tightly behind him. He looked through the front of the van, trying to figure out which police station they were heading for. The squad car in front indicated right and Danny braced himself for the turn. To his surprise, the car peeled off while the van continued on straight. Swinging his head round to look out the rear window, Danny watched the navy Transit turn right after the squad car, leaving him alone with the two men in the front of the riot van.

'Oi, dickhead, where are we going?' he shouted.

The driver didn't answer. He just put his hand up and adjusted the mirror, bringing two eyes into view as they stared at him. Danny noticed a crude tattoo on the back of the man's hand as he moved the mirror. It was a V with a star over the top. It reminded him of something from the past. He just couldn't put his finger on it. One thing was for sure, it didn't look like a tattoo a policeman would have, more like a prison tattoo.

The vehicle drove on until Danny recognised the buildings and roads that ran between Heathrow's many airport terminals. It eventually drove up an industrial park next to the airport and stopped outside a small unit with *KLV Air Freight Services* across the top. Within a few seconds, the roller door opened. A burly, thickset guy with a blond crew cut coming into view as he pulled on the chain to raise it. The driver put the riot van into reverse and manoeuvred it inside the unit. Danny watched as the roller door lowered behind them. He prepared himself for the worst, refusing to let fear get the better of him. If he died, he died. He'd faced death many times and accepted the fact he'd escaped its inevitability more times than he should have. The back doors opened, and the big guy looked in at Danny in the caged section as the driver joined him.

'You sure that's him, Ivan?' he said with a strong Russian accent.

'Yeah, I'm sure, Pasha, the boss sent us a picture before the grab,' replied the driver also with a Russian accent.

'He doesn't look like much,' said Pasha.

'Let me out of this cage and I'll fucking show you what I look like,' growled Danny.

'Ha, that's the spirit. Go to sleep now, tough guy. You're going to need the rest where you're going,' said Pasha, pulling a tranquilliser gun out of his jacket and firing it at Danny's arm before he could move.

'Fuck off y—'

The drug hit him like a ton of bricks, sending him into darkness in seconds.

'Ok, let's get him out and into the livestock crate. He's on a cargo plane to Moscow with some prize goats at eleven o'clock,' said Pasha.

Ivan unlocked the cage and he and Pasha picked Danny up and carried him to a large wooden crate in the warehouse. Leaving him cuffed, they placed him inside and put the lid on, nailing it shut before walking away.

'Here, this is the address to get rid of the van,' said Pasha, handing Ivan a piece of paper and an envelope full of money. 'Ask for Billy and give him the money. He knows what to do. When you're done, get a taxi to the airport. We leave for Moscow this afternoon.'

The two men smiled at each other before Pasha went to the front of the unit and raised the roller door. Ivan hopped in the riot van and drove it out and away down the road. Pasha stood in the open doorway watching him leave, before pulling out his phone and making a call.

'*Da*, it's me. The package is all ready. Come pick it up now.'

'On my way,' came a curt response before hanging up.

Thumbing through the contacts, Pasha made another call.

'Yes,' came a cold reply.

'It is done. We have him. They are coming to collect him for the plane now,' said Pasha.

'Thank you, Pasha. Your loyalty to my father and to me will not go unrewarded. See him on the plane, then come and pick me up from the hotel,' said Annika, still without a hint of emotion.

'Yes boss,' was all Pasha said in return.

CHAPTER 8

After quickly clearing security at the entrance to the Secret Intelligence Service, or MI6 building as it was commonly known, Howard took the lift to the top floor and headed for the office of the Chief of the Secret Intelligence Service, Edward Jenkins. He knocked as he entered, standing silent for a minute as Edward finished a call.

'Do we know which station he's at?' Howard asked as Edward put the phone down.

'No, we don't,' said Edward with concern.

'Well, there must have been an arrest warrant raised and a custody record somewhere?' said Howard, a little irritated.

'No, there isn't. That was the Commissioner of the Metropolitan Police. There is no warrant for Danny's arrest on any police system and no authorisation for an armed response unit to Scott's address.'

'What about the police van, 52, CP20?' said Howard, pacing up and down the office, his mind doing overtime.

'The van went missing from the vehicle compound at Lewisham police station last night, and surprise surprise, they had a CCTV malfunction last night, so there is no footage of the disappearance,' said Edward sitting back and waiting for Howard to speak.

'I don't like it, Edward. As an asset, Daniel and myself may not always see eye to eye. But he's my asset and the best one I've got. I want him back, no matter what it takes,' Howard said, stopping his pacing to face Edward.

'Ok, what have we got to go on?' said Edward, leaning forward in his chair as Howard finally took a seat.

'A couple of days ago, I sent Daniel to Paris, a simple information exchange. The job was a setup. The target was Daniel himself, but not a hit. They were planning to kidnap him,' said Howard, his tone informative, not emotional.

'I see, that does put a different view on things. So this was a planned second attempt that would seem to have been more successful.'

'Exactly. Now, the Paris job was the result of information passed to me by the Minister of Defence, James Bullman. Apparently, he was contacted by the man in Paris asking for money for information regarding an inside man who's been selling Ministry of Defence weapon designs to the Middle East. It may have been a legitimate contact, but I have the minister under surveillance as a precaution. One thing that does strike me as suspicious is our minister called Police Chief Superintendent Terence Crawford late last night,' said Howard, pausing to note Edward's raised eyebrows.

'Mmm, yes, very. So you think our minister called in a favour and the chief organised an off-book grab,' said Edward, thinking out loud.

'It certainly looks that way, but without any evidence we can't pull the Minister of Defence and Police Chief Superintendent in. I'd have half the House of Lords and the Prime Minister on my back before we got them out of the car.'

'Quite. Ok, I'll handpick some men and we'll get digging,' said Edward.

'We need to find where that van went. It's a police riot van, for God's sake. It can't be that hard to find,' said Howard, turning to leave.

'I'll call you as soon as I have something.'

'Thank you, Edward. I knew I could count on you,' said Howard, marching out the door.

'No problem, you're not the only one who owes Daniel for saving their life,' said Edward, his words stopping Howard in his tracks.

He turned and gave Edward a nod of understanding, then continued on his way.

Reaching for the secure phone on his desk, Edward punched in a number.

'Gregg, it's Edward. Can you and your team meet me in incident room eight in an hour? I have a job for you. Highest priority.'

'Yes boss, we'll be there in an hour,' came Gregg's reply.

He hung up and sat back again, thinking. A minute or so later, he reached for the phone once more.

'Hi, Trevor, this is Edward Jenkins. I'm after a favour.'

'Yes, Mr Jenkins, what can I do for you?'

'All police vehicles are GPS tracked aren't they,' he asked.

'Yes sir.'

'Good. A riot van from Lewisham went missing last night, and I'd like to know its movements,' said Jenkins.

'Have you got the vehicle ID, sir?'

'Yes, it's 5, 2, Charlie, Papa 2, 0.'

'Got it, I'll get on to police control and get back to you.'

'Thank you, Trevor,' said Jenkins, getting up to prep the incident room for the investigation.

CHAPTER 9

anny woke in darkness, the deep throbbing hum of the old Boeing 777 Global cargo plane's jet engines penetrating the crate and hurting his foggy head. While the last remnants of the drug wore off and his eyes adjusted, he moved his cuffed wrists under his bum and hooked them over his feet so his arms were free in front of him. Running his hands along the inside of the crate, he tried to work out the size and material of the box that contained him. As he moved forward, little beams of light shot past his side, illuminating the other side of the crate by his feet. Turning, Danny discovered two rows of air holes behind him. Placing his eye to one of the holes, he could see the large cylindrical interior of the cargo plane.

There were a number of crates beside his one. Danny imagined they were the same as the one he was in. If he listened closely he could hear the odd bleating noise. Sheep or goats. Definitely livestock. He breathed a sigh of relief. The cargo hold would be pressurised and heated, so at least he wouldn't freeze or suffocate in transit.

With his head clear, his body flexing, and his mood darkening, Danny studied the goat crates through the air holes. They were made from half-inch pine and held down by two heavy duty luggage straps fixed on the long side of the crate, across the top and down the other side. He squinted, trying to get a focused look at the fixings on the corners of the crate.

Be nails, please be nails.

He finally got a clear look at one of the round fixing heads and was relieved to see it was smooth, no slot or crosshead of a screw.

Great, end of the crate it is then.

Shuffling onto his back, Danny slid as far as he could until his shoulder blades were wedged up against one end of the crate. Drawing his legs back until his knees touched his chest, he tensed and relaxed, taking in great gulps of air to force as much oxygen into the blood as he could, ready for an explosive move. Unleashing every ounce of muscle power, Danny thrust his legs forward, powering his heels into the end of the box. The thud reverberated through his body, pushing his shoulders painfully into the wood behind him.

No movement.

With the goats bleating in panic at the sudden noise, he breathed heavily, sucked in more precious oxygen and repeated the process. This time the crate made a dry creak and a tiny shard of light came in through a millimetre gap between the end panel and the side, as the smooth-sided nail was knocked out a bit. If it had been screwed down, the thread would have gripped the wood and it would have held fast. He powered his legs into the end panel a second time, and the crate gave another dry creak as the nails gave up another five millimetres of hold. The third blow powered the panel off on one side, bending the nails on the other, leaving the panel swinging open like a jagged hinged door.

Sliding himself out, Danny stretched and took in the cavernous interior of the cargo plane. Looking down at his handcuffs, he pondered his next problem. At the front of the plane, next to the bulkhead door and the pilot's cockpit, sat a large metal lock box with cargo manifests attached to clipboards above it. He made his way over and opened the lock box. It was full of luggage straps and wooden chocks, a crowbar and a small toolbox with pliers, side cutters and screwdrivers. Picking up a luggage strap, Danny pulled up the metal clasp and looked at the split pin that held its hinge in place. Taking the pliers out of the toolbox, he held the clasp between his feet while bending the ends of the split pin straight and pulling it out of the hinge.

After five minutes of struggling with the pliers and side cutters in cuffed hands, he straightened the pin out and fashioned a small hook in the end. Once that was done, he sat on the box and placed the hook of the pin into the handcuff lock. Closing his eyes, he concentrated on feeling the pins inside. The lock picking skills he learned in the SAS were a bit rusty, and it took him twice as long as it should have, with his hand bent back in the cuffs to reach the lock, but eventually it clicked and the cuffs opened. He rubbed his wrists then took one of the cargo manifests off the hook. He frowned at the destination of Sheremetyevo International Airport, Moscow. His mind ticked with the thought of the Russian in London and the tattoo on his hand, the V with the star on top. A Volkov Mafia tattoo.

Years ago, when Danny had just left the SAS, Danny's uncle, Harry Knight, had got caught up in a power play for London by the Volkov Russian Mafia family. The conflict had been bloody, with family members getting killed on both sides. It ended when Danny killed the heads of the Volkov family, Sebastian and Yuri, at their ancestral estate just outside Moscow.

As if on cue, the aircraft banked gently to one side and started its final descent. With his mind going ten to the dozen, Danny looked over at all the cargo. Taking it all in, he grabbed the crowbar from the lock box and started to move.

CHAPTER 10

Sitting in a large van in the car park, Karl and Ustin watched the Boeing 777 Global cargo plane through the chain-link fence as it landed then taxied out of sight behind the cargo terminal.

'Is that the one?' said Ustin, nodding towards the plane.

'So my brother says. Where's that fucking farmer?' said Karl, craning his head to check the rest of the car park.

Bang on cue, a mud-covered old farm truck drove noisily into the car park. It stopped beside them in a cloud of diesel smoke, its green canvas-covered rear full of sewn-on repair patches. The weather-worn face of the farmer looked across and nodded to them from the cab.

'Ok, he's here, let's go,' said Karl, turning back to Ustin.

They got out and headed into the terminal, with the farmer shuffling along behind them.

'May I help you?' said the young attendant on the desk.

'Are you Andre?' said Karl, barely acknowledging the man as he stared intently into the office behind him.

'Eh, no. But I can help you, sir,' he replied nervously.

In the office a middle-aged guy looked up, startled. He hurried out to the desk area as fast as he could.

'It's ok, Lesta, I will deal with these gentlemen. Can you go and get the goat crates ready for dispatch by the loading bay, please?' Andre said hastily.

'Ok, but don't we have to open and check them first?' said Lesta, a puzzled look on his face.

'No, it's fine. Just do as I ask, please,' said Andre, a little more urgently than he intended.

Lesta didn't question his supervisor further, he just turned and disappeared through a door to the warehouse.

Karl gave Andre a big grin when Lesta had gone, his cold eyes and gold tooth glinting in the harsh lighting, sending a chill down Andre's back. He leaned in, making Andre flinch, and pulled out an envelope with a big wedge of rubles inside, sliding it across the desk. Andre grabbed it quickly and shoved it in his pocket as he looked around nervously to make sure no one was watching.

'Drive up to the gate and I'll let you into the loading compound.'

Karl and Ustin turned to leave without a word. The old farmer gave Andre a toothless grin and followed them out. The two vehicles drove up to the gate as it drew back for them to pass through. Karl backed the van up by the large loading door, while the farmer did the same beside them. Both killed the engines and hopped out as the metal roller door opened. They opened the backs up as Andre appeared and directed Lesta on a forklift as he loaded the goats onto the farmer's truck.

'No, not that one, that's for the other van,' shouted Andre over the chug of the forklift as he pointed at the crate with a V on the side. The farmer, fresh with his envelope of money, waved at Karl and Ustin and drove off in a cloud of diesel smoke as they shut the back of the van. Ignoring him, Karl got in and drove out the gate. Hearing movement in the back, Ustin swung around in the passenger seat to look at the crate.

'I think he's awake.'

'Ha, he's going to wish he was still asleep when they've finished with him in Lefortovo Prison,' said Karl, laughing.

'Baa—baa,' came the shriek of a goat from the crate.

'What the fuck?' shouted Karl, stamping on the brakes.

The sudden movement only made the goat bleat more.

'Oh, this is bad. The boss and your brother will go mad when they find out,' said Ustin, his face falling at the thought.

'Annika and Pasha are not going to find out. That idiot Ivan must have put him in the wrong crate. Listen, they don't land for a few hours, we'll catch up with the old man and get the Englishman back before anyone finds out,' said Karl, jamming the van into gear and flooring it out of the car park.

'Which way did he go?' said Ustin as they approached the junction.

'I don't know. I'm sure he's from somewhere near Sloboda. You've got his number, call him. Call him now,' Karl shouted at Ustin.

'Ok, ok, I'm calling,' said Ustin, fumbling with his phone.

He pressed call and put the phone to his ear, frowning as it rang and rang until the answer phone kicked in.

'Hey, old man, you've got our crate. Call me the second you get this, you hear me, the second, ok?' he said hanging up. 'Shit.'

'Fuck, how far could he have got in that rusty piece of crap?' said Karl, driving the van as fast as it would go.

Ustin's mobile ringing made them both jump.

'It's him,' said Ustin, looking at the screen.

'Well answer it then, hurry.'

'Hey, farmer, where are you? You've got our crate,' said Ustin, feeling a sense of relief at contacting the old man.

'I'm just passing Kapotnya oil refinery,' said the farmer.

'Ok, find somewhere to pull over.'

'There's a junction up ahead, just past the refinery. I'll pull off there and wait for you.'

'Good, we are on our way,' said Ustin, turning to Karl. 'He's in Kapotnya district by the refinery.'

Karl cut across two lanes of traffic and screeched the van around, the revving diesel engine drowning out the bleating of the startled goat in the back.

CHAPTER 11

Danny let the side of the crate drop out. After dragging the protesting goat by the horns and pushing it into his crate, Danny had nailed a luggage strap to the inside of the goat's crate and held it in place while they loaded it into the farmer's truck.

As soon as the decrepit truck left the airport he climbed out and took a deep breath. Clearing the smell of goat piss and shit from his nose, Danny looked around the back of the old farm truck, which didn't smell a hell of a lot better. He made his way to the rear and pulled the canvas flaps aside so he could see out. The truck was moving in a flow of heavy traffic as it passed a massive oil refinery on the outskirts of Moscow. It peeled off the motorway and drove along the outer perimeter of the refinery, finally pulling up in a lay-by next to row after row of six- and eight- storey, run down, grey concrete apartment blocks built in the Cold War era.

Still in his running gear, Danny hopped down, turning his head at the sound of an approaching van. Although he hadn't seen Karl and Ustin before, the stunned looks on their faces as they got eyes on him left him in no doubt that they were here for him. As their brakes screeched, Danny took off across the road, running at full pelt down the tree lined pathways between the apartments.

———

'Fuck, that's him,' shouted Karl, jumping on the brakes as he watched Danny hop down from the farmer's truck, stare him in the eyes and take off.

'What the fuck are we going to do now?' said Ustin, watching the toothless farmer walk to the back of his truck scratching his head.

'It's ok, he has nowhere to go, the refinery fence is on this side and the river Moskva on the other, this is the only way out of the estate,' said Karl, pulling a Makarov pistol out of his jacket as he climbed out of the van. 'Get on the phone, get everyone here NOW. We need to get this bastard before Annika and Pasha touch down.'

'Ok, ok, I'm on it. What about the police commissioner? He's on the payroll.'

'Good idea, Ustin, get him as well, get everyone.'

———

Danny flew through block after block, easing back into a good running pace. His first thought was to put as much distance as he could between him and the truck and van. He figured he was dressed in running gear, so act like a runner. His second thought was to get to a phone and contact Howard. He needed to get out of Russia and find out who was out for the revenge of Yuri and Sebastian Volkov's deaths.

Leaving the depressing grey of the apartment blocks

STEPHEN TAYLOR

behind, Danny followed a path through the trees. His heart sank as he emerged to find the wide Moskva River ahead of him. He looked right for a way out. The high security fences of the oil refinery cut off his exit. He looked left and the river curved around the estate, disappearing under a bridge with the busy motorway on top. No exit that way. The river itself was too wide and flowed too fast to swim across. Angry and frustrated, Danny turned, looking back through the trees at the tops of the apartment blocks. His eyes went dark and his face set like granite.

I'm going to have to fight my way out the way I came in, and those fuckers know it.

CHAPTER 12

Within twenty minutes cars were screeching into the estate. Karl sent men along the embankment beside the motorway in case Danny tried to make it across. He sent the rest of the men into the estate, driving slowly through the crisscross of roads with their guns on their laps as they tried to spot him. Minutes later police cars and a couple of riot vans drove into the estate, sirens wailing and blue lights flashing. The commissioner stopped his car by Karl's van. He got out and shook Karl's hand before signalling to his men. They disembarked the vehicles and swept into the estate.

'Remember, we need him alive,' he shouted after them.

'Thank you. Miss Volkov will be most appreciative, Commissioner,' said Karl, noting a greedy twinkle in the commissioner's eye.

'It is a pleasure to be of assistance to Miss Volkov,' he said, standing to attention before giving a curt nod and following after his men.

Heading back through the trees, Danny looked up and down the empty road before crossing it. He headed for a gap between two buildings and was halfway across when a black Mercedes 4x4 appeared between two apartment blocks to his left.

Why do the bad guys always have black 4x4s?

Darting his head in the other direction, two Russian police officers moved around the far end of the other block. His first thought was to hand himself in and call Howard from the safety of a Moscow police station. That thought went out of his head the second he heard the men from the Merc shouting to the police officers. They immediately looked at Danny and went for their guns.

Danny didn't speak Russian but was damn sure they weren't saying, 'Welcome to Moscow, have a nice day.' He took off between the two buildings and came out into a recreational park, surrounded on all sides by six-storey grey concrete apartment blocks. He had a really bad feeling about how this was going to play out.

The park was empty; no kids, no mums with prams and toddlers. In the apartment windows, he saw people backing away and a mother frantically dragging her child through the entrance of the block to his right. A quick glance behind him confirmed that the officers were giving chase, one shouting down his radio while the black Mercedes whizzed away on the road behind them.

Danny ran towards the far corner and the alley leading out between the buildings. As he entered it, two more policemen blocked his exit. Using his speed and momentum, Danny kicked off the concrete wall and spun a powerful kick to one officer's head. At the speed he was moving, the blow sent the man flying sideways, landing in a crumpled heap, out cold on the ground. Stunned, the other officer shouted something in Russian and went for his gun.

Landed from the kick and moving in one fluid motion, Danny grabbed the gun before he had time to level it, twisting it out of his grip while his other hand grabbed the man by the balls, gripping them like a vice. The man's face went purple as he froze, unable to breathe, and in too much pain to move. Danny dumped him into the bins and carried on running, aware of the footsteps from the first two officers growing louder behind him. Leaving the alley, Danny flattened himself against a wall. He calmed his breathing and listened. He heard the guy climb out of the bins, loud and clumsy as he tried to get a breath through the pain in his crotch; he heard the two other police officers run into the alley, shout something in Russian to the downed man before heading his way. Concentrating on the sound of the footsteps, Danny tensed his legs and held his arms up, gun in hand, ready.

Nearly. One, two.

He swung round fast and chopped the policeman in the throat with the butt of his handgun, knocking him backwards into his partner, sending them to the ground.

'Give me your phone, er, mobil'nyy telefon,' Danny shouted in his limited Russian, pointing his gun at the floored officer lying next to his choking partner.

Moving his hands slowly, the officer gripped the top of his phone and pulled it out of his pocket, passing up to him. Taking it, Danny tucked it in the elastic of his running shorts then reached down and snatched the handcuffs off the officer. He threw them at him, pointing the gun at them, indicating for the two men to cuff themselves together. As soon as he heard the cuffs click locked, he took off again. Tucking the gun in the back of his shorts, Danny pulled the phone and started tapping in a number. Only half looking where he was going, Danny headed through the recreational area of the next set of accommodation blocks. The phone rang for a frustratingly long time before clicking on to the answerphone as Danny ran out the far side of the block and across the road.

'Hi, this is Scott Miller. I'm otherwise engaged at present. Please leave a message and I will get back to you shortly.'

'Scott, it's me, Danny. I don't have much time. Get hold of Howard and tell him I'm in Moscow. I've been kidnapped by the Vol—'

The conversation was cut short by a screech of brakes. He just had time to jump up, saving his legs from the impact as the bumper of the Mercedes went under him. Danny's backside hit the front windscreen, shattering it as he bounced up in the air and somersaulted over the roof of the car, disappearing out of sight as he fell to the ground behind it. His phone flying off in one direction and the gun in another.

CHAPTER 13

'Oh shit, you better not have killed him, Stefan,' said Igor, as the two men sat in the car, stunned.

'The bastard just ran out in front of me. There was nothing I could do,' replied Stefan, turning around in his seat, trying to see Danny.

'You try telling the boss that and you'll find yourself at the wrong end of Pasha's gun,' said Igor.

'If he's dead we say nothing, you hear me, Igor? We get back in the car and drive off. Ok?' said Stefan, fixing Igor with a not-to-be-argued-with stare.

Igor nodded in agreement, gripping their guns. The two men tentatively opened the car doors. Climbing out, they moved slowly towards the back of the vehicle. They swung round at the same time, pointing the guns at the empty tarmac.

'Where the fuck did he go?' said Igor, looking across at an equally puzzled Stefan.

'Shit, he couldn't have got far,' replied Stefan.

———

The second Danny hit the ground, his survival instinct went into overdrive. He fought off the shock and pain and fast-crawled under the car, thankful for the high ground clearance of the 4x4. He froze when the doors opened and feet hit the road on either side of him. As soon as they moved towards the back of the car, Danny crawled out the front and popped up into a painful crouch. He peeped around the side to see Igor with his back to him looking at the empty road behind the car. Springing forward, Danny covered the length of the car in two steps. He opened his hand wide, swung his arm in, catching Igor's head like a catcher's glove catches a baseball, powering it sideways into the side of the Mercedes.

As the impact boomed and Igor's head bounced off the bodywork, Danny did a spinning back kick, knocking the surprised Stefan's gun out of his hand. With his adrenaline in full flow, Danny didn't feel the bruising pain of his impact with the car. He launched a lightning combination of punches, ending with a full-on blow to Stefan's face, flattening him and his nose as he went down and stayed down.

Leaving them, Danny ran forward and closed the passenger door before heading around the front to get in the driver's side. He heard shouts from behind him as he slid into the driving seat. More police emerged from behind the apartment blocks, guns drawn as they approached. Danny dumped the car into first and floored the accelerator, tearing up the road before handbrake turning and heading in the direction of the motorway.

Come on, come on. I've gotta get out of here.

A few hundred metres further on, Danny screeched the Mercedes around another corner, holding it at the limit of its grip as he joined the road that he'd entered the estate on. The farmer's truck had gone, but the van was still there, surrounded by parked police vehicles. Luckily, they were hunting a man on foot and hadn't blocked the exit road. Changing up a gear, Danny flooring it again, charging past the van and scattering police officers as he overtook their parked cars and vans.

Just as thoughts that he was going to make it dared to enter his head, Danny's eyes were drawn to a figure emerging from behind a parked police van. He moved like a bowler as he slid a stinger across the road. Danny was too close and travelling too fast to avoid it. The tyres deflated with a succession of bangs as they ran over the rows of spikes, leaving the vehicle impossible to control. The rim of the rear wheel caught the kerb, kicking the Mercedes off the road and into a ground-floor apartment, stopping it dead in a cloud of concrete dust, glass and splintered wood. Danny tried to brace himself, but his momentum against the sudden stop was too great. His chest slammed into the steering wheel and his head smacked into the windscreen with a hefty thud. Flopping back in the driving seat, Danny looked around, his vision blurred and ears ringing. Shapes of people approaching the car and muffled shouts barely registering. He was vaguely aware of the door opening before his eyes rolled back in his head and he lost consciousness.

CHAPTER 14

'Thank you,' Scott said, signing for a parcel at the entrance doors to his apartment building.

He hopped into the lift and took it back up to his apartment floor. Closing the door behind him, he put the package on his office desk and wandered through to the kitchen to grab a coffee. He noticed a missed call from an international number he didn't recognise, and a voice message notification on his mobile. Scott clicked on the voice message, putting it on speaker while he pressed the button on his expensive built-in coffee maker and grabbed the milk to steam into the perfect latte.

'Scott, it's me, Danny. I don't have much time. Get hold of Howard and tell him I'm in Moscow. I've been kidnapped by the Vol—'

The message startled Scott, causing hot milk to slosh over his hand.

'Damn, blast,' he yelped, as the little stainless container clanged off the kitchen floor.

After running his hand under the cold tap, Scott played the message again. He didn't have the high-level government man's number, so he called Danny's boss, Paul Greenwood.

'Greenwood Security, how may I help you?' came a woman's cheerful response.

'Hello, my dear, could I speak to Paul, please? It's a matter of great urgency,' said Scott, his reserved English manner stopping him from shrieking down the phone.

'Who may I say is calling?' came the highly proficient response.

'Scott Miller.'

'Please hold one minute,' she said.

It didn't take one minute. Paul was on the phone in a couple of seconds.

'Scott, nice to hear from you. What's so urgent?' said Paul with polite curiosity.

'I've had a message from Daniel and need to get hold of Howard.'

'Ok, I can do that. What was the message?' said Paul, talking to Scott on the office phone while he tapped out a message on his mobile and hit send.

'What? Er, he said he's been kidnapped and to get hold of Howard. Oh, and he is in Moscow,' said Scott, turning his head towards a knock on the apartment door. 'Hang on, Paul, there's someone at the door. Paul? Hello? Hello?'

With Paul gone, Scott put the phone down and wandered to the door. Looking through the spy hole, he was surprised to see Howard standing on the other side.

'Howard, how?' Scott stammered as he opened the door.

'Good afternoon, Scott. Be a good fellow and make me a coffee from that wonderful machine of yours,' said Howard, walking past Scott with a smile as he made his way into the apartment.

'Er, yes, of course,' said Scott, confused as he followed Howard into the kitchen.

'I believe our missing friend has been in contact,' said Howard, gesturing towards Scott's phone on the kitchen counter.

'Yes, unfortunately I was downstairs signing for a parcel when he called. He left a voice message. Here, I'll play it to you,' said Scott, hitting play before cleaning up the spilled milk and attempting to make another coffee for himself and a fresh one for Howard. When the message had finished, Howard sat at the breakfast bar and picked up Scott's phone.

'May I?' he said, shaking it at Scott.

'Be my guest, old man. The pin is 2903,' Scott said, placing a coffee next to him.

Howard unlocked the phone and checked the missed call and voice message before tapping and forwarding it. He placed Scott's phone down and made a call on his own.

'Edward, I've just sent you a secure message from Scott Miller's phone.'

'Yes, I'm playing it now. Moscow. The kidnapped bit with the cut-off part name Vol. Are we thinking a possible Volkov connection?'

'Mmm, it's been a long time since anyone's mentioned that name. We don't have anything else to go on, so let's get on to our contacts in Moscow and see what we can dig up. Also, get onto the mobile network and get a location for Daniel's call. I'll be back soon,' said Howard hanging up.

He slid Scott's phone back towards him and raised his cup in thanks.

'You're welcome. May I ask a question?' said Scott, looking nervously at Howard.

'Ask away.'

'How come you were here the second I called Paul?

Are you watching me?' Scott said, shuffling from one foot to the other.

Howard took another sip of coffee and put the cup down, smiling. 'Not at all, my good fellow. I was already here. I have a team downstairs going through the building's CCTV footage. We are trying to identify the policemen who grabbed Daniel.'

'Oh, I see, of course, sorry,' said Scott, relaxing.

'Don't mention it, and thanks for the coffee. Now I really must go. I've got a man to find,' said Howard, pointing to Scott's phone as he drained his coffee cup, stood up and made for the apartment door.

He said his goodbyes as Scott saw him out. He took the lift down to the foyer where he was met by two of his men.

'Everything ok, boss?'

'Yes, I'm heading back to headquarters. Pack it up. I'm pulling surveillance on Mr Miller. We have a new lead to follow.'

'Yes sir.'

Leaving the building, Howard's car pulled up beside him as he approached the road.

'Headquarters please, Frank,' he said, climbing into the back seat.

'Yes sir.'

CHAPTER 15

Waking up with a start, Danny sat bolt upright, the blinding pain in his head making him instantly regret it. After several deep breaths, the pain subsided to a constant throb and the stars in his vision faded enough to take in his surroundings. He was on the top bunk of a metal framed bed, in a ten-by-ten-foot cell with a barred window above a stainless steel toilet at one end and a grey painted, heavy steel door at the other end. Blinking away more stars, Danny looked down at his navy blue trousers and jacket with white and blue striped bands around the ankles and wrists.

'You finally awake, English?' came a deep voice from below.

Danny peered over the edge to see two thick muscular legs swing out from the bunk below. The top of his long-haired head on broad, powerful shoulders followed until a stocky man with classic Russian features stood looking at him.

'Let's get one thing straight, you're the last fucking person I want sharing my cell. You do whatever I say, bitch, and I won't fuck you up, you understand?' he said through gritted teeth, his index finger jabbing at Danny from a heavily tattooed fist.

Danny's vision cleared and the pain in his head dulled. He jumped down from the bunk, landing solidly on his feet. Standing stock still, Danny's eyes locked unwaveringly on the cellmate in front of him.

'Where am I?' he said in a low growl.

'Hey, piece of shit, you don't talk unless I tell you to. Got it?' the man said, his face angry, his finger jabbing at Danny again.

Quick as lightning, Danny grabbed the finger and snapped it back, dislocating it at the knuckle, before throwing a powerful jab to the man's stomach, knocking the wind out of him and sending him stumbling back to dump down on the toilet seat. He sat there red-faced, staring at his finger in disbelief as he struggled to get his shocked diaphragm to suck in any air.

'Now you listen to me. I've had a pretty fucking shit day. Ok. Now you fucking do whatever I say or next time I snap your neck like a twig. Got it?' Danny said through gritted teeth while he leaned in on the man, his face like granite, staring with dark, dangerous eyes.

'Ok, ok,' the man managed to wheeze in response.

'Give me your hand,' Danny said without moving back.

The man nervously did as he was told. Danny grabbed the finger and pulled it out and down with a loud click, popping the knuckle back into place.

'Argh, fuck,' the man yelled, shaking his hand as Danny let go.

'Right, let's start again shall we? Where am I?'

'Lefortovo Prison, Moscow.'

'What's your name?'

'Leonid Turgenev,' Leonid said, his breathing starting to return to normal as he eyed Danny cautiously.

'Do you know why I'm here?'

'No, but Sarkis and the *V*'s on B-Wing got real excited when they heard you were coming,' said Leonid, rubbing his knuckle and relaxing a bit.

'The Vs?' said Danny, hoping his suspicions about the answer weren't going to be right.

'*Mafiya*, er, Volkov Mafia, Sarkis Kiselyov is their head man in here,' said Leonid, his face snarling as he spoke, followed by a spit on the floor at the mention of the Volkov name.

'But the Volkovs are finished, dead, gone,' said Danny, moving back to sit on the edge of the bottom bunk.

'They were until Yuri Volkov's bastard daughter came of age and inherited her father's empire. Over the past couple of years she's pulled all of Yuri's contacts and men together and paid, threatened or murdered the Volkov Mafia empire back to life.'

'And your beef with the Volkovs?'

'Eh, what is beef?' said Leonid, looking confused.

'Sorry. Argument, er, problem with the Volkovs.'

'Since the end of the Second World War, my family has been at war with the Volkovs. We ran the north of the city. They would kill one of ours. We kill one of theirs, it's the way it's always been. When the Volkovs were murdered and the estate burned down, we took control of Moscow and the surroundings areas and that's the way it has been for five years. Then it all changed. Annika Volkov hit us out of the blue with all of Yuri Volkov's old crew, led by Pasha Manolov, hired mercenaries and a Moscow Chief Police Commissioner on her payroll. We didn't stand a chance. All our men were hit or arrested. My father and brothers were killed. I was ambushed by the police as I got into my car; they'd planted a weapon in the glovebox and fitted me up for a murder, so here I am. Which is why I didn't want you in the same cell as me, I have to watch my back in here, I can't be babysitting someone else on the Vs hit list,' said Leonid, wincing as he stood from Danny's punch to his stomach.

'I don't need babysitting, but if you watch my back, I'll watch yours,' said Danny, his face deadly serious as he extended his hand.

Leonid looked at him, rubbing his belly while he opened and closed the fingers on his sore hand.

'*Da*, ok. Is good idea. What is, er, beef with the Volkovs?' said Leonid, ignoring the pain as he shook Danny's hand.

'Five years ago the Volkovs tried to take over London. They killed my aunt and kidnapped my cousin, then put a hit out on me, so I killed them all,' Danny said, his face expressionless and voice calm.

Leonid's face fell as Danny's words sunk in. 'Holy shit, we heard the rumours the English had driven them out and killed them, but we never knew for sure. How did you end up here?'

'I was drugged and kidnapped in London. Next thing I know, I'm here,' Danny said, touching the painful bruise on his face.

'They didn't kill you for a reason, probably the same reason they sent me here.'

'And what's that?' Danny said, his interest piqued.

Leonid lifted his shirt to show a multitude of scars depicting slashes, stabs, and burn marks. 'Annika Volkov's revenge. The Vs are paid to hurt me any way they can, but they're not allowed to kill me. The infirmary patch me up then the Vs put me right back in there, it's a constant living hell. Now get the fuck off my bed,' he continued, holding his gaze for a couple of seconds before breaking into a wide grin.

Danny gave him a smile back. 'Perhaps it's time we even the score,' he said, getting up off Leonid's bed and hopping back up onto the top bunk.

CHAPTER 16

The men on the iron gates let Karl and Ustin into the large shingle drive that led up to the Volkov mansion. They parked next to the numerous builders' vans belonging to the glaziers and painters and plumbers still working on the final stages of the build. Annika had been determined to build the mansion on the site of the old Volkov family estate, a defiant statement to all that the destruction of the old estate by Danny Pearson on the night he'd killed the head of the family, Sebastian Volkov, and Annika's father, didn't mean the end of the Volkovs power over Moscow.

'Don't say anything stupid, Ustin, leave the talking to me, ok?' said Karl, feeling nervous after being summoned to the estate by Annika, but glad to have his brother's protection.

'Fuck off, Karl, I'm not a fucking idiot,' Ustin snapped back grumpily.

They both fell silent when the front door opened and the formidable figure of Pasha stepped out. He stared at them, his forehead creased in an unimpressed scowl. He turned without speaking and walked inside, knowing the two would be following close behind. As he entered the kitchen, he stepped to one side, letting Karl and Ustin pass him into the room. They stood stock still at the sight of Annika on the far side of the room. A loud tap echoed off the marble floor as she walked in her stilettos with her back to them, checking the large bifold doors as a group of nervous glaziers continued to fit them. She clicked to a halt and spun around on her heels to face Karl and Ustin. Her long blond hair dragged into a tight ponytail, swished as her ice-blue eyes locked upon the two men.

'Leave us,' she said abruptly.

The window fitters looked up, unsure of who she was addressing. Pasha stepped forward menacingly, cocking his head to one side to indicate for them to get lost, which they hurriedly did.

'Well,' she said coldly.

The two men stood dumbfounded, not knowing what they were supposed to say.

'Let me help you out. When were you going to tell me you lost him and had to get the police commissioner in to get him back?' she said, her voice direct and unemotional.

'There was a problem with the crate. I thought it best to use everyone to get him back,' said Karl apologetically.

'What problem?' Annika replied, her heels clicking on the marble as she paced up and down.

'It wasn't our fault. Fucking Ivan put him in the wrong crate. He went off with the farmer while we had a fucking goat,' Ustin blurted out before Karl could answer.

One of Pasha's shovel-sized hands was on the back of Ustin's head before he could say any more. With terrific force, Pasha drove Ustin's head down, cracking it onto the edge of the white marble worktop of the kitchen breakfast bar with a sickening thud. Gripping Ustin's hair, Pasha pulled his head up and rammed it back down again. He did it over and over, getting faster each time. A crimson smear appeared on the white surface until Ustin's skull fractured and the smear became a spreading puddle before Pasha dropped Ustin's limp body to the ground.

'Would you like to explain that again, Karl?' said Annika, no hint of shock or emotion at the ferocity of Pasha's attack.

'It's true. Somehow he got out of the marked crate and switched with one of the goats. Maybe on the plane, I don't know. You were still in the air, so I had to use everyone I could to get him back,' said Karl without expression.

The room sat in silence as Annika maintained her stare. A trickle of sweat ran down the side of Karl's face as Annika reached inside her handbag.

'Ok, I believe you,' Annika said pulling her phone out, dismissing the subject as she clicked her way towards the exit.

As Pasha shook his head, Karl let out a sigh of relief.

'Get rid of that, Karl, and clean up my new kitchen,' Annika said as she left the room.

'Your mess, brother. I'm not going to help you,' said Pasha, walking after her, leaving Karl alone with Ustin's body.

'I told you to keep your mouth shut, you fucking idiot,' he muttered to the bloody mess on the floor.

Annika walked out of the mansion towards the car. Ivan opened the rear door for her, closing it after she slid gracefully inside. He moved round and got in driver's seat as Pasha got in the front beside him.

'Take us to the prison, Ivan. I want to see how our

guest is settling in,' Annika said, pulling the hem of her dress straight as she relaxed in the back.

'Yes boss,' said Ivan, driving smoothly towards the gate, nodding to the guards as they opened them and watched them drive through.

CHAPTER 17

'How are we doing, Edward?' said Howard, entering one of the SIS building's incident rooms.

'Ah, morning, Howard,' Edward replied, writing something on one of the various whiteboards. 'Well, we know where he was 24 hours ago. The cell information put his call in a housing estate in the Kapotnya district of Moscow, here,' said Edward, moving to another board and pointing to a circled area of a satellite map.

'Anything else?'

'Yes, hang on. Tim, can you put that footage up on the main screen please?' Edward said to one of the agents tapping away on a computer terminal behind them.

'Yep, coming up now.'

The large flatscreen TV on the wall burst into life with some shaky footage, obviously filmed on a phone out of an apartment window. It was shot looking across a road at the walkway between two grey concrete apartment blocks. Two Russian policemen ran into the walkway as Danny came into view on the far side, still in the shorts and T-shirt from outside Scott's apartment. He ran at full pelt before springing off the wall to kick one of the approaching policemen into a crumpled heap on the floor, then tackling the other policeman by the balls to get his gun. Edward and Howard watched in silent awe as Danny proceeded to take out two more policemen before getting hit by a car, and still managing to take down the two armed occupants before driving off.

'I've always known he was good, but until you see him in action, it's hard to appreciate exactly how good he is,' said Edward, waving at Tim to pause the footage.

'Quite, which is why we must get him back. Can we go back to the car please?' said Howard, turning to Tim.

The video played backwards past where Danny got in, past where he kicked Stefan's gun out of the way, past crashing Igor's head into the roof of the car, to where the two men got out of the vehicle.

'Stop there, please. Back a touch, that's it.'

The freeze frame showed Stefan and Igor's faces fairly clearly as they got out and headed for the rear of the car.

'Enhance the images and run them through the computer please. Let's see if we can get some names. Where did the video come from?'

'A Facebook feed from a kid in one of the apartments,' said Edward.

'Very good. Any more news about who snatched him outside Scott's apartment?'

'We're still looking for the riot van. But we got some footage off the CCTV in Scott's apartment block foyer. It's not great, but as far as we can tell, the armed police unit was real. As there is no authorisation for the arrest, we're going through shift rotas to see where all the members of the Met's armed units were at the time. We're also checking the armoury logs to see who signed out weapons,' said Edward in his usual methodical manner.

'Excellent. Anything on Chief Superintendent Crawford and our Minister of Defence, Mr Bullman?' said Howard, checking his watch.

'Nothing yet.'

'Ok, keep me informed. I'm off to Moscow,' said Howard, turning to leave.

'On your own?' said Edward, his eyebrows raised.

'No, I'm taking Tomas Trent and John Ball with me. I have a rather delicate meeting with a Russian counterpart to attend. He may be able to shed some light on the whole affair,' said Howard, leaving the room without waiting for a reply.

Climbing into his chauffeur-driven car, he had Frank drive him to his government office, known only to a very select few.

'Wait here, I'll only be a few minutes, Frank,' he said, getting out and marching up to the solid looking entrance door.

He looked up at the camera mounted above the entrance. The lock buzzed to let him in before he had a chance to look down. Moving up the stairs at an energetic pace, he entered the office and stood between the analysts, looking at the main screen.

'Any news, Martin?'

'Nothing new, boss. The minister's hardly been in the office, William's been delving into his finances looking for any anomalies but nothing as yet.'

'Thank you, Martin. I'm going to be out of town for a while. Let me know if you find anything, and copy Edward Jenkins in on any progress,' said Howard, spinning on his heels to leave. 'Encrypted communications only, please, Martin.'

'Ok boss,' Martin shouted after Howard as he left the office.

CHAPTER 18

Walking confidently into the prison reception area, Annika passed the waiting line of visitors to the reception desk and cut in front of a man as he stepped forward to the desk.

'Hey lady, get to the back of the queue,' he said, reaching his hand forward to grab her shoulder.

Pasha's vice-like grip caught his wrist and folded his arm back.

'You do not touch the lady,' he said leaning in, his face hard and full of menace.

'Ok, ok,' the man said, withering at Pasha's aggression.

'Annika Volkov, I'm here to see the governor,' she said, tapping her perfectly manicured nails on the Formica counter.

'Go straight through. Someone will escort you inside,' the receptionist said, buzzing the lock on the security door.

They walked through into a large room with inspection tables for searching bags, and floor markings for people to stand on for body searches. Two prison officers moved in front of Annika and Pasha, halting their progress.

'Bags and personal belongings on the table, please, then stand on the blue mark,' one of them said moving behind the desk, ready to search Annika's bag.

Annika walked straight past him, heading for the entrance door to the prison, with Pasha close behind.

'Hey, back here, bags and personal belongings on the table and get on the blue mark,' the man yelled while his colleague moved swiftly to block the door.

Pasha moved in front of Annika, his body tense as his face hardened.

The entrance door behind them opened swiftly as another uniformed man hurried out. 'Hey, whoa, Pavel, it's ok, let them through,' he shouted, beckoning Annika and Pasha over.

'This way, please, Miss Volkov,' he said, leading the way.

'Thank you, Mr Lebedev. I trust you got your payment and everything is in place,' Annika said, clicking along the corridor slowly, forcing Lebedev to slow down and listen to her every word.

'Yes, yes, Sarkis is waiting to welcome him when they go to the dining hall,' Alek Lebedev said in a hushed voice, his eyes darting along the corridor to make sure nobody was listening.

'Very good. I will expect a full report.'

'Yes, of course, Miss Volkov.'

They walked in silence, pausing here and there to unlock the various heavy metal doors and barred gates until they arrived at the governor's office.

'Come in,' Boris Oblonski yelled from inside after Alek knocked.

'Ah, Miss Volkov, what a pleasure to see you again. Come take a seat. Can I get you anything, tea, coffee?' he said smiling, while his eyes followed Pasha nervously as he walked in behind Annika and remained standing upright by the door.

'No,' Annika said coldly.

She moved forward in the awkward silence that followed, smoothed her dress, and sat in the chair on the opposite side of Boris's desk.

'Leave us, please, Alek,' Boris said, watching him leave, closing the door behind him.

Annika remained quiet as she stared like a hawk at its prey. Sweating nervously, Boris seemed to shrink in his chair as he waited for Annika to speak.

'Thank you for accommodating our guest, Mr Oblonski. His welfare is of great importance to me. I want him to suffer greatly in here, but he must not die,' she said. As if on cue Pasha stepped in, a look of menace locked on his face.

'Er, I, of course. I will keep an eye on things personally,' stuttered Boris, eyeing Pasha.

'Perfect, I hope Mrs Oblonski is enjoying the new house?'

'Yes, we're both very happy there,' said Boris, relaxing a little.

'My pleasure,' she said, standing to leave.

'Sorry, yes, thank you,' Boris said, moving around the desk to see her out.

He didn't want to upset his most generous benefactor to the charity fund for prisoner rehabilitation, a fund that had paid for his new house.

'Goodbye, Governor, and remember, he must not die, not until I say so,' Annika said, her heels clicking off the hard floor as she left the office, walking deliberately slowly towards Alek who was waiting by the locked exit gate.

Pasha turned slowly, eyeing Boris with contempt as he left.

Unnerved, Boris returned to his desk, slumped down in the chair and slid open the bottom drawer. He drew a bottle of vodka out with a shaky hand and poured himself a small shot. Downing it in one, he gave a sigh of relief, then poured another one.

CHAPTER 19

'What the hell is he shouting about?' said Danny, turning away from the black and purple bruised image in the polished steel panel that served as a mirror on the cell wall. An angry prison officer was yelling from the communal area outside their cell.

'It's dinner time. Come, we go,' said Leonid, walking past him.

'Mmm, steak and chips would go down nicely,' Danny said, following Leonid and the rest of the prisoners headed for the dining hall.

'Stick close to me, do as I do and sit where I sit,' Leonid said in a hushed voice over his shoulder.

They moved into a large hall with eight-man metal tables and benches bolted to the floor in straight lines. Danny moved behind Leonid, his eyes facing forward to the serving area at the front of the line. His concentration was in his peripheral vision as he noted eyes following him around the room. Copying Leonid, Danny grabbed a plastic food tray with six sections and a flimsy plastic spork, a cross between a spoon and a fork, purposely too brittle to cause anyone damage and only just strong enough to eat food with. He slid the tray along the stainless steel rail in front of the servers where a fat, bald-headed guy missing his little finger unceremoniously dumped grey-looking potatoes and something mildly resembling a stew on his tray. Keeping close to Leonid, Danny walked confidently towards a bench. A thin guy with glasses looked up, nodded and said something in Russian to Leonid who sat next to him. Danny sat opposite, still very aware of the tension in the hall his presence was causing.

'So this is him?' said the guy with glasses, smiling at Danny.

'Yes, this is him, but you'll have to speak English. He doesn't know any Russian,' Leonid said, pulling a face as he took a mouthful of stew.

A big guy with Leonid's features dumped his tray on the bench with a bandaged hand and sat down next to Danny. He grinned, making the scar in the corner of his mouth crease its way up to his cheek. Tensing, ready to block and move, Danny stared at him with dark, menacing eyes.

'Hey, relax, is my cousin Valerik, and this is Filip,' Leonid said before saying something in Russian to them both.

'It is an honour to meet the man who killed Yuri Volkov,' Valerik said, slapping Danny on the back.

Danny gave him a nod and continued eating. The food was rank, but old habits from the SAS were kicking in: eat and drink where you can, the body needs fuel to fight. Leonid's body language changed. He stiffened and his attention was elsewhere, looking at something behind Danny.

'Sarkis has just passed something to one of his men.

72

He's getting up, coming this way,' Leonid whispered to Danny.

'Short guy, something in his right hand,' Danny replied, his eyes narrowed, locked on the reflection of the approaching man in Filip's glasses.

'Da.'

Danny's hands gripped the sides of the plastic tray. He tensed his muscles, ready to move, his mind calculating the man's steps before the attack. If they'd been told not to kill him, it'd be a stab low on the right side.

Three, two, one.

Twisting fast on the bench, Danny spun the tray up like a crap shield, stew and potatoes spraying all over the floor as the man's razor-blade-melted-into-the-end-of-a-toothbrush banged into the hard plastic before dragging off loudly as he drew it back for another attack. By this time Danny was up on his feet. He kicked the knife wide while bringing the plastic tray up. With a powerful thrust, Danny banged the back of the tray into the man's face before headbutting his way through it, snapping the tray in half as he made contact with the bridge of the other man's nose. His attacker went down like a felled tree, his eyes rolling back in his head as blood poured from his broken nose. Danny just stood there, gravy trickling down his face, staring defiantly at the man who'd passed the knife to his attacker. Valerik kicked the makeshift knife under the table to Leonid, who covered it with his foot.

'Sit, English, sit. Filip, the tray,' he whispered, pulling Danny onto the bench seat as Filip slid his tray over.

'Take the knife and go, quick,' Leonid said to Filip, who immediately reached down and slid the knife from under Leonid's foot and tucked it into his sock before scooting off as prison officers noticed the man on the floor.

Banging his baton down on the metal tabletop, the officer yelled at Danny, 'You, what happened here?'

When he didn't get so much as a blink, the guard raised his baton and went to strike him. Danny's hand shot up, catching the baton in a steely grip.

'Hey, cut him some slack, eh. The man doesn't speak any Russian,' Leonid said hastily, with his hands up to pacify the guard.

Danny stared at him a second or two longer before releasing the guard's baton.

'What happened to him?' he said, ignoring Danny and pointing to the unconscious guy on the floor being attended to by the other guard.

'The stupid fuck slipped on this fucking awful stew. He banged his head on the bench as he fell,' said Valerik, leaning around Danny to grin at the guard.

An uneasy silence fell upon the table as the guard looked from man to man to man.

'Back to your cells,' he eventually said gruffly.

They got up. Valerik tapped Danny's arm and nodded for him to follow them. As they left the hall, Danny caught Sarkis's hateful stare from the other side of the room. They maintained eye contact until Danny passed through the door and made his way back to his wing.

CHAPTER 20

'So what's the plan, boss?' said Tom, enjoying the first-class seat and the free drinks handed out by the attractive British Airways stewardess.

'Plan is a very fluid term right now, Tomas. Once we have checked into our hotel, I'd like you and John to take a little look around the area where Daniel was last seen. I have a meeting with an old acquaintance who might be able to help us,' said Howard, sipping his scotch on the rocks.

'One of ours?'

'No, most definitely one of theirs. Very big in the former KGB. I don't think he has a formal title these days,' Howard said with a wry smile.

'Oh, a Russian, Howard,' Tom said, grinning back.

'Something like that,' Howard said as the plane pitched for its descent into Sheremetyevo International Airport.

They landed and cleared customs. Howard took the lead, marching off to the Avis desk to rent a car. As Tom stood with John, waiting, he saw Howard hand over a driving licence and passport for the car hire with the name

Bernard White on them. He wondered briefly if that was the government man's real name, but decided that was highly unlikely. Howard drove skilfully through Moscow without the aid of satnav or directions, obviously familiar with the city, although Tom and John knew better than to ask him why. After checking into the Hotel Metropol just off from Moscow's famous Red Square, Howard gave Tom and John the car keys and sent them off to check out the Kapotnya district housing estate.

Turning, Howard walked back into the hotel foyer. He passed reception and the selection of sofas as he headed for the hotel bar. He paused by a man sitting in one of the comfy sofas, his head hidden behind a newspaper.

'Good afternoon, Lem, care for a drink?' Howard said cheerily.

The top of the newspaper flipped down to reveal a silver-haired man with classic Russian features and piercing, sky-blue eyes. 'I thought you'd never ask. Nice to see you again, David, or is it Howard these days?' he said, a wide smile spread across his face.

'It is, but what's in a name, my friend?' Howard said, as the man stood and shook his hand before embracing him.

'How true. Now, how about that drink? I'm intrigued to know what's so important for you to fly all the way to Moscow,' Lem said, following Howard to a seating area away from prying eyes.

'What can I get you?' said a pretty waitress when they were settled.

'Vodka on the rocks,' Lem said with a smile.

'Gin and tonic, please,' Howard said in perfect Russian.

'The years have been kind to you, my friend. You look good,' said Lem, making idle chat until the waitress returned with their drinks.

'As do you. The FSB has served you well,' said Howard,

pausing the conversation as the waitress placed their drinks on the table.

'Let us not play games. You know I am no more FSB than you are MI6. What is the purpose of your visit?' Lem said the moment the waitress had gone, his smile dropping as his face turned serious.

'Ok, I'll get to it then. I have a man missing in Moscow.'

'A spy?' Lem said, matter-of-fact.

'No, he was kidnapped in London and brought here. Last contact was from an estate in the Kapotnya district. Here, we found some footage from a Facebook feed,' Howard said, tapping his phone before handing over the video of Danny.

Lem watched it in silence, his forehead creased with concentration.

'He is good, very good.'

'He is, and I want him back,' said Howard, taking the phone back.

'Any idea who took him and why?'

'Five years ago we both had a problem with a family not very far from here. You supplied me with information, and I took care of it. To be precise, the man in the video took care of it,' Howard said, taking a sip of his gin and tonic.

'The Volkov's. I have been hearing rumours about their return. Yuri's daughter, Annika, has been reviving her father's empire. The one in the video who gets his head bashed against the car is Igor Popova. I know of him,' Lem said, looking up at Howard.

'Will you help me find my man?'

'I owe you for five years ago. I will repay my debt. But you and the two men came with must keep a low profile. Moscow is a very corrupt place and the Volkov's are very well connected. Send what you know to my private mailbox. I will do what I can,' said Lem, downing his drink before getting up to leave.

'Thank you, old friend,' said Howard, standing to shake Lem's hand before he walked out of the bar.

CHAPTER 21

itting outside the cell in the communal area while Valerik and Filip played chess, Leonid gave Danny a nudge and nodded his head to the far side of the cell block.

'That's Alek Lebedev, prison warden. Watch him, he's bad news,'

he whispered.

'One of Volkovs'?' Danny whispered back.

'Yeah, he's on the payroll for sure.'

Danny eyed the man up at the other end of the room. He was a big guy, fit, about Leonid's size, with similar colour hair cut into a crew cut.

'How tall do you think he is?' Danny said curiously.

'Er, what, I don't know, 180, 190 maybe, why?'

Danny paused for a minute while he did the maths. 'Mmm, 6-foot to 6-foot-2. Pretty close,' Danny muttered, more to himself than anyone else. 'Just running through options,' he finally said.

'Options, what the fuck do you mean, options?' Leonid

said. Across the table Valerik stopped mid-move to look at him.

The siren rang once to signal lockup time and disrupted the conversation. The prisoners got up and shuffled their way to their cells. Taking their cue, Danny got up and followed behind Leonid to their cell. He'd just got inside when a heavy blow caught him in the kidneys. As he went down on one knee, more blows cracked across his back. Danny twisted to get his arm up in defence, only to feel the hard metal baton whack down on his forearm.

'Annika Volkov sends her regards,' Alek Lebedev said in broken English.

He swung at Danny a few more times, catching him on the side of the head, sending him to the floor with flashing stars dancing in front of his vision.

'Stay where you are, Turgenev, unless you want the same,' Alek said, pointing the baton at Leonid as he backed out of the cell, slamming the heavy door shut behind him and locking it for the night.

Rolling onto his back on the floor, Danny breathed heavily as he waited for the pain to subside.

'Bastard. You alright, English?' said Leonid, swearing in Russian towards the locked door.

Holding his side, Danny slowly got off the floor and sat on the bed. He touched the side of his head with his other hand, taking it away to see blood on his fingertips.

'He's going to regret that,' he finally said, his face steely and his eyes dark and menacing.

'Yeah, good luck with that,' said Leonid, damping down a bundle of toilet roll and handing it to Danny.

'Thanks,' Danny said, dabbing at the blood seeping through his unruly mop of wavy brown hair.

'This is what it's like for us in here. You just try to survive,' said Leonid, shrugging.

'Not for long, Leonid. I haven't quite figured it out yet but we're getting out of here, and then I'm going to make them pay.'

CHAPTER 22

The phone rang in the Minister of Defence's office as James Bullman was packing up for the night. He contemplated ignoring it, but his fear of missing something by not answering got the better of him.

'James Bullman,' he barked down the phone.

'James, it's Terence,' said Police Chief Superintendent Terence Crawford.

'Ah Terence. What can I do for you?' James said, sounding more interested than he actually was.

'It's about your bloody favour. I've got MI6 agents and Internal Affairs looking at shift rotas and staff profiles. It's only a—'

'For Christ's sake, not on this line, call me on my private number,' James shouted, slamming the phone down before Terence could say any more.

Seconds later the mobile in his pocket rang, not the one he usually used, the one he kept for private things; things nobody other than him should ever know.

'What the hell are you doing ringing me on an unsecured line?' James berated Terence before he could get a word out.

'Er, sorry. With all this going on I just can't think straight. If they find out, if one of the team talks, I'll be finished. We'll be finished,' Terence said, his voice pitchy as he talked fast.

'Pull yourself together, man, just let me think. Mmm, how many men were in the armed raid?' James said, calm and collected.

'Five, all handpicked,' Terence said, his speech slowing as he calmed down.

'How vulnerable are we?'

'They're going through everything, rotas, weapons and vehicle logs, it's only a matter of time before they work out who could have been at the grab site,' Terence said, the panic starting to rise in his voice again.

'Then we'll have to take them out of the equation,' said James, his voice cold and emotionless.

'What do you mean, take them out of the equation?'

'Don't be so bloody naïve, Terence, you know exactly what I mean.'

'No, I can't. This is insane,' Terence said, taken aback at the suggestion.

'Listen, you snivelling little shit, you didn't mind when I cleaned up your mess with that poor girl at university, did you, and you damn well didn't mind when I helped you get the chief superintendent position, so bloody well do as you're told and I'll make this go away, ok?' James said raising his voice again.

The line went silent for a while.

'Ok, sorry, James,' Terence finally said, defeated.

'Get your men on shift tomorrow. There'll be a call out. I'll send you the details in the morning. It'll look like a raid gone wrong and nobody will be any the wiser,' James said, already mentally choosing the asset to deal with this.

'But what about MI6 and—'

'Goodnight, Terence.'

'But—'

'I said goodnight, Terence,' James said more forcefully, before hanging up.

He pocked the mobile and looked at the office phone the chief superintendent had initially called him on.

He'll have to go.

Frowning, he looked around the office before reaching down and opened the desk drawer. He took out a large Manila envelope. Opening it, he slid out the CCTV stills of his indiscretions at the Volkov's London brothel all those years ago. Tipping the envelope up, he shook the memory stick containing the video footage of him out onto the desk and twiddled it in his fingers.

At least I'm finally free from that bitch's blackmail.

Tucking the contents back in the envelope, he put his jacket on and tucked the envelope in his inside pocket and left.

———

Not too far away inside Howard's London office, Martin, William and Brian worked frantically at their computers, separating the multiple audio tracks from bugs and phone taps in the minister's office. They enhanced the audio and transcribed the one side of the conversation between John Bullman and Terence Crawford into text, then sent it to Howard and Edward's encrypted mailboxes.

'Get onto the Chief Superintendent's phone provider and find out what number he called when Bullman answered his mobile. I want to know that number within the hour so we can get a tap on it,' said Martin to the others.

'Already on it,' came William's response.

'The boss is going to want to pull out all the stops for sure,' said Brian, seeing a reply from Howard seconds later.

"Get everyone on Bullman and Crawford. I want to know every move they make, who Crawford's team members are and where their little house clearing exercise is going to take place."

'Green light, guys, wake 'em all up. We need eyes and ears on these guys like yesterday. Martin, can you sort two mobile tech units? You and I will go mobile on each target and liaise with William back here, ok?' said Brian, pulling up the asset list and reaching for the phone.

'Yep, on it,' shouted Martin from the other side of the room, the excitement of a live operation electrifying the office.

———

Exiting the lift, James Bullman headed to the security desk in the foyer.

'Excuse me.'

'Yes sir,' the security guard said, looking up from his monitors.

'Has my office been swept this week?'

'Er, let me see,' he said, pulling up the log. 'They did it on Tuesday morning, sir.'

'Mmm, could you have it done again, please, er ...?'

'Nigel, sir.'

'Nigel, thank you. Any issues report directly to me,' Bullman said, turning to walk through the metal detector and leave.

'Yes sir. I'll attend to it straight away,' Nigel said,

speaking to Bullman's back as he marched out the entrance doors.

CHAPTER 23

Danny went from asleep to heart-stopping awake in a split second. Something was wrong. He looked down towards his feet to see the cell door wide open. The dull night lighting from the communal area outside cut its way into the cell, just strong enough to light it up in a jaundiced yellow-grey light. Rolling to one side, Danny dropped to his toes and rolled down onto his heels while bending his knees, landing without making a sound. He tapped Leonid on the shoulder, clamping a hand over his mouth when he awoke with a start. Placing a finger to his lips, Danny took his hand off Leonid's mouth and pointed to the open cell door.

———

At the far end of the cell block, the prison warden, Alek Lebedev, unlocked the barred gate before turning and walking away without looking back. Seconds later, Sarkis Kiselyov and two men walked cautiously to the gate and eased it open. Holding pillowcases loaded with heavy soap bars, they scooted quietly into the communal area, heading past the locked cell doors in the dim light, stopping short of Danny and Leonid's open cell door.

'Where the hell is Sasha? He's supposed to be keeping watch,' Sarkis whispered, looking around. 'Never mind. Come, we do this now.'

The three men wrapped the tops of the pillowcases around their knuckles, shortening the distance to the hard bars of soap in the other end, making it easier to thump them down like a cosh. They moved silently to the cell door and looked in at the top bunk. An evil grin crossed Sarkis's face at the sight of Danny moving under the covers in the yellow-grey gloom. Following his lead, they moved inside as fast as they could and powered the pillowcases into soft flesh, the soap bars thudding brutally into the body like being hit with hammers. The body in the bed jerked and rolled, a muffled cry coming through from under the covers.

Sarkis put his hand up to make the others stop, then whipped the covers back. His eyes went wide at the sight of Sasha writhing in agony on the bunk, his arms tied behind his back with the sleeves of his top and his mouth gagged with a pair of socks. Before they could turn, Danny and Leonid flew in through the cell door. With the speed of his forward motion amplifying the power of his punch, Danny struck Sarkis on the side of the head with a sledgehammer blow. Sarkis flew into the end wall and slid down onto the stainless steel toilet, out cold. Behind him, Leonid kidney-punched one of the men, grabbing the other around the neck as the first one went down, choking him to the ground.

The punched man recovered quickly. He jumped upright and swung his loaded pillowcase wildly around until it hit Danny on the back of his neck. Turning slowly,

Danny's face contorted into a steely snarl, his dark eyes invisible in the gloom. The man instantly withered at the menace in front of him, dropping the pillowcase and holding his palms up in front of him in an attempt to pacify him. No such luck. Exploding out of the shadows in an uncontrollable rage, Danny destroyed the man with a blistering combination of punches, still hammering blows into him as he lay on the floor semiconscious.

'Hey, Danny, stop,' Leonid said, his voice raised as loud as he dared. 'Stop, don't fucking kill him, you'll have us both in isolation on a murder charge.'

When Danny didn't stop, Leonid grabbed him around the neck and pulled him back. Still enraged, Danny spun, his fists raised, ready to strike. His face softened at the last minute as recognition kicked in. He lowered his fists as they looked at the unconscious and writhing men around them. By this time, the noise had woken other prisoners on the block and the yells and banging on the cell doors was ramping up.

'We gotta move. The guards will be here any minute,' Leonid said, grabbing the unconscious man by the legs.

———

Running to the barred gate ahead of the guards, Alek Lebedev pretended to unlock it before pulling it open for the six prison guards approaching behind him. All the lights in the block came on as they caught up with him.

'Follow me,' Alek said, running towards Danny and Leonid's cell.

He stopped dead, confused at the sight of Sarkis and one of his men unconscious on top of the table tennis table in the communal area. Sarkis's other two men writhed about in agony on the floor beside them. Alek looked over at Danny and Leonid's closed cell door. He faltered for a few seconds, not knowing what to do. Shaking it off, he walked up to the cell door, inserted his keys and pretended to unlock it while obscuring the view to the guards behind him. Drawing his baton, Alek stood to one side, ready to charge in as one of the guards pulled it open. He halted anticlimactically at the sight of Danny and Leonid lying in their bunk beds. Their heads popped up and looked passively at Alek as they sat up with just-woken-up looks on their faces. Doing a bad job of hiding his anger, Alek moved out of the cell, slamming and locking the door shut behind him. From inside, Danny and Leonid could hear him shouting at the guards to get the prisoners to the infirmary and wake the doctor. After a few minutes, the noise outside their cell died down and the harsh strip light protected by a metal cage on the ceiling clicked off, leaving them in darkness once more.

'Hey, English, what's this plan of yours to get us out of here?'

CHAPTER 24

I n his oak-panelled home office in the prestigious St John's Wood area of London, James Bullman addressed the last few pressing emails before packing it in for the night. His phone rang as he fired off the last response.

'James Bullman,' he barked.

'Sorry to bother you, Minister, it's Nigel on security.'

'Yes Nigel.'

'We've done a sweep of your office, sir, and I'm afraid we found three devices. Would you like me to contact Scotland Yard for you?'

'No, it's fine. It's part of a security initiative. Well done, Nigel, you've done well. Er, leave the devices in situ, I'll decommission them myself in the morning,' said James, lying with well-practised political ease.

'Very good, sir, thank you,' said Nigel, beaming with pride at the rare compliment.

'Yes, yes, good night, Nigel,' said James, impatient to get the man off the phone.

'Good night, sir,' Nigel said, finally hanging up.

This changes everything. What did I say to Terence? What exactly did I say?

James sat concentrating on the conversation from the moment the office phone rang to the conversation on his private mobile.

Nothing that would hold up. I didn't mention names, places. No, I'm fine, but tomorrow's plans require a change.

He pulled the little black address book from his jacket pocket, opened it, and grabbed his private mobile. As he started to make a call, he stopped mid-dial and stared at it, thinking. Grabbing it in two hands he bashed it on the edge of the desk, snapping it in two. After dropping it in the bin, he slid the desk drawer open and pulled out a brand new pay as you go phone still sitting in its blister pack wrapping next to his Smith & Wesson M&P 9 handgun. Tearing it open, he dialled a number from the address book.

'Hello,' said the voice on the other end.

'It's me. Plans have changed. I have new targets,' said James, a smile creeping across his face at his own brilliance.

'Go on,' came the calm monotone response.

CHAPTER 25

'Morning, gentlemen,' said Howard, already at the breakfast table sipping his coffee while reading the Kommersant Russian newspaper, a half-eaten pastry in front of him.

'Anything good, boss?' said Tom, taking a seat.

'Mmm, residents near a government facility on the outskirts of town are complaining of headaches and nausea after some sort of emergency at the facility. Several dead and more injured were taken to hospital with multiple haemorrhages and organ failure. Rumours of a pulse weapon test gone wrong have been strongly denied. How very intriguing. Anyway, how did you two get on yesterday?' Howard said, folding his paper neatly and placing it on the table.

'Well, we found the car Danny drove off in,' said Tom, looking up at the stained-glass dome covering the roof of the large, ornate, centuries-old dining hall.

'Sterling work, gentlemen. Any sign of our missing friend?'

'Don't get too excited, boss, it was embedded in the

front of an apartment block as we entered the estate. No sign of Danny, and a fair amount of dried blood on the dash,' said John, looking across at the breakfast buffet and china plates with a frown.

'Anything else?' said Howard, smiling at the two of them looking at the selection of Russian breakfast choices on offer.

'Er, yes. We went to see the kid who took the film. Turns out he speaks excellent English and loves the UK, posters of the Beatles on the wall and everything. Anyway, we told him we were reporters doing a story on social media and Russian kids. The kid gets all excited when we ask him about the video and starts showing us a whole load of social media from him and his mates on Mafia brutality, killings and businesses burnt out. He tells us there's been a big turf war between the Turgenev family and the Volkov family. Apparently the Volkovs came out on top. As for the police, he said, 'Police no good, the Mafia own the police.'

'Well, at least that confirms our fears. Our only problem now is, if he's still alive and where he is?' said Howard, waving a waitress over for more coffee.

'Can Russian Howard help us with that?' said Tom, pausing to order coffee for him and John on top of Howard's order.

'Yes, Tomas, I'm hoping so,' said Howard, a faint look of amusement on his face at the use of Russian Howard.

'Good. Now, I'm starving, point me towards the full English breakfast,' Tom replied.

'I'm afraid it's pastries, pancakes, caviar and salmon, or a selection of cold meats,' Howard said, tipping a nod towards the buffet spread.

'Christ, not much of a holiday, this, is it,' said Tom, heading for the pancakes.

'What do you want us to do today, boss?' John said, pointing to the pastries as Tom loaded a plate up for him.

'Nothing. We wait to hear from my contact. You and Tom go and do some sightseeing, Red Square is only a short walk from here.'

'And what are you going to do, boss?'

'The London team has a lead on the armed police team that grabbed Daniel outside Scott's. It appears the men in charge are going to try to silence them in some staged raid gone wrong. So when the UK wakes up in an hour or so, I will be on video call to HQ for as long as it takes,' said Howard, checking his watch for UK time.

'Here you go,' said Tom, dumping a plate piled high with pancakes and pastries on the table, much to the disgust of the well-to-do diners sitting on the table opposite, eating petite slices of caviar and salmon.

'Oh, and boys, try not to get into trouble while you're out and about,' Howard said dryly.

CHAPTER 26

The rest of the night had been quiet after Sarkis and the V's' failed attack. The guards segregated the prison blocks at breakfast, doubling-up on manpower in case trouble flared up between the groups. Danny looked but couldn't see Sarkis or any of his men.

'Leonid says you have a plan—'

'Crazy plan,' interrupted Leonid.

'A crazy plan to get out of here,' said Valerik in a hushed voice.

'Not here, we'll talk later in the exercise yard,' said Danny, taking a cautious look at the flicking eyes and turning heads at the table next to them.

Valerik turned around and gave them a withering, warning stare, turning them back to their food with heads down.

'Fuck them, they are nothing,' he growled.

'Not here, cousin, listen to Danny, we talk later,' said Leonid, grabbing Valerik's arm.

'Ok, ok, we talk later,' said Valerik, turning back to his grey-looking porridge.

The rest of breakfast passed in silence. They got up and split to their relevant blocks where they waited until the claxon finally sounded and the guards moved them all out to the exercise yard. Danny made a mental note of all the gates and doors leading to the yard, trying to piece a plan of the prison together in his head from his movements between the block, the dining hall, and the exercise yard. He also took a note of which direction the guards went when they left at the end of their shift, counting the minutes until they were replaced by the next shift.

The yard was situated dead centre of the prison, surrounded on three sides by the walls of C, D and E blocks. A fifteen-foot wall topped with great spirals of razor wire spanned the fourth side. Four crude, netless basketball hoops sat equally spaced at either ends of the tarmacked yard. Close-knit gang members played around their own hoop, while the others in their gang sat on benches behind them, giving hateful stares to a mirror-imaged rival gang on the other side.

Danny instantly caught sight of Sarkis and the V's on the far side, sitting on three-tiered concrete steps, with Sarkis on the top tier. Sasha and the two guys who attacked their cell sat beside him while nine other V's sat across the two lower steps, completing the pyramid of power. All four men of the top tier zeroed in on Danny and Leonid, watching them from bruised and beaten faces. Sarkis watched with one hateful eye; the other was blackish-purple and still swollen shut. To Leonid's surprise, Danny gave them a wide smile and a wink before turning away.

'You're one crazy bastard. Sarkis looks fit to explode,' Leonid said, tracking the V's looks over Danny's shoulder.

He continued to watch a few seconds longer, just to make sure Sarkis wasn't heading across for an attack. When they stayed put, Leonid turned and sat on an identical set of concrete steps on their side of the yard. A minute or so later Valerik and Filip entered the yard and headed over to sit on either side of them.

'Well, what's this plan?' Valerik said, leaning in with a hushed voice.

'Him,' Danny said, looking straight ahead at Alek Lebedev as he patrolled on the far side of the yard. He paused by Sarkis and said something to him before giving Danny a sideways glance and continuing his patrol.

'What do you mean, him?' Valerik said, confused.

'How far is the nearest hospital from the prison?' said Danny.

'Er, I don't know. The general hospital is around a mile away, why?'

'If a warden and a prisoner got seriously injured, what would happen?' Danny said, his eyes following Alek Lebedev as he chatted with another guard in the far corner of the yard.

'They would phone for an ambulance and take you to the infirmary to wait for it. Then you go to hospital,' said Valerik, while Leonid shook his head.

'Which, at a mile away, would be here in under five minutes, right?'

'Right.'

'And they would take the prisoner straight out of here to hospital,' said Danny, turning to look at Valerik.

'Ah, I know what you're thinking. It wouldn't work. You would be handcuffed to the stretcher and they would send a guard with you.'

'Yep, but they wouldn't handcuff the injured warden, would they?' Danny said, breaking into a grin.

'I don't get it. How is this going to help you?' said Valerik, frowning.

'You give Leonid a haircut, put him in the warden's uniform and cover his face in blood like he's been badly injured. No one would question it, he's the same height as the warden, same hair colour, same build. As soon as we're in the ambulance, Leonid takes out the other guard and unlocks me and we get the hell out of there,' said Danny, his confidence making a convincing case for the escape plan.

'You see, Valerik, I told you, it's a crazy plan. They would get the doctor to check you out before they call the ambulance, and there would be at least four more guards when the alarm is raised,' said Leonid still shaking his head.

'Mmm, he is right. Once the alarm is raised one of the other guards is bound to figure out Leonid's not the warden,' said Valerik, frowning.

'Ok, ok, scrap that then. What comes in and out of this prison?' Danny said, his mind already clicking through possibilities.

'Eh, food supplies, but they are all searched in and out. The guards, obviously, and a garbage truck comes in every Tuesday for the bins,' said Valerik, racking his brains to think of options.

'A garbage truck, what if we could get in that? They can't search it,' Danny said, turning serious again.

'Nah, me and Valerik worked the kitchens. We've seen it come and go. They tip the bins in and then hit the button for the hydraulic compactor while the guards watch. You'd be crushed to death,' said Leonid, dismissing the idea.

'But we could stop the compactor with something, a brace or iron bar,' said Danny, ticking the idea over in his mind.

'Yes, it might work. The lorry would drive straight out of here. But you'd still be trapped in the back of the garbage truck. You could be crushed by the next load, or suffocate,' said Valerik, shaking his head.

'Mmm, we'd need a man in the garbage truck to make that work. Ok, any other ideas?' Danny said to blank faces.

CHAPTER 27

One of the nine screens burst into life as Howard's laptop logged on to his London base's encrypted connection.

'Morning, boss,' said William, tapping away at his own workstation as he talked over the headset.

'Morning, William. What's the state of play?' said Howard, wanting to get up to speed as soon as possible.

'Ok, let me see,' said William, tapping rapidly over his keyboard. 'Screen share coming up now. This is a shift change request late last night. It brings five members of an armed response unit together. Four of them were not working the morning of Danny's kidnap and are on our list to find their whereabouts at that time.'

'Who requested the shift change?' said Howard, already knowing the answer.

'Chief Superintendent Terence Crawford, sir,' replied William.

'Mmm, what about the fifth member?'

'That's where it gets interesting. We found no arms logged out to account for the time of Danny's kidnap, and we were beginning to think the kidnappers were not police at all. That was until I checked the fifth man's whereabouts on the day in question. He was standing in for the armoury clerk who was off sick that day,' said William, dropping the screen share to bring Howard's face back.

'How very convenient. Where are the teams?'

'We've got one team ready to detain the men as they leave New Scotland Yard once the callout has been made. Brian is in a tech van, ready to lock down the kill site. We're thinking some sort of IED booby trap to take the five men out, possibly a sniper to take out any survivors,' said William, getting a thumbs-up from Brian on a camera feed to one of the other screens.

'Excellent, and what of our esteemed Minister of Defence, Mr Bullman?'

'Martin is in the other tech van with a tracking team keeping tabs on James Bullman. Nothing of interest to report as yet.'

'Ok, we'll have to get the bugs out of his office sharpish; when his little plan to eliminate the armed response team goes awry he'll be on his guard and have the office swept,' said Howard, more thinking out loud than giving the order.

'Already done, boss. Lionel going in with the cleaning crew early hours to remove them.'

'How very forward-thinking of you, William. Well done. We'll have a chat when I get back. I think a review of your pay grade may be in order,' said Howard with a smile.

'Yes, boss, thank you. Oh hang on, we've got the call coming in now. Armed unit to attend, gun shots reportedly heard from an old shoe factory in Lewisham. Alpha team, go, go, intercept the armed response now. Brian, I've sent you the address. Mission is a go.'

'Affirmative, we're en route, ETA 15 minutes,' came Brian's voice over the revving of the tech van.

'I'm patching you into the live camera feeds now, boss,' said William, buzzing off the operational excitement.

They watched as various vehicle cameras and body cameras showed a speedy drive through London's crowded streets, and armed men in black tactical body armour bouncing around as the vehicles cornered hard.

'The armed response team has been detained. The boys are escorting them to the SIS building for questioning,' came a voice over William's computer.

'Thank you, Simon. Edward Jenkins is expecting you.'

The next five minutes flew by in tense silence. The vehicles reached their destination and braked hard outside the old abandoned factory, the front and rear vehicles turning sideways across the road to block any passers-by.

They watched as the team moved either side of the entrance door, letting two others through with a heavy battering ram. It took a couple of knocks before the wood around the door frame split in two and the door blew inwards. Standing back, the other members of the team swept into the building, their Heckler & Koch MP5 submachine guns up and ready as they moved through the interior in close formation, entering the rooms carefully as they looked for tripwires or pressure plates, anything that might indicate an IED trigger. After ten minutes they found nothing and started to work their way out again.

'Place is clean,' came Brian's voice from the tech van.

'Ok, wrap it up,' said William, shrugging to Howard through the camera.

'I don't like this, William, I don't like it one bit. Someone's playing us for fools,' Howard said, a frown crossing his face as he looked past William on the camera feed. Two figures had entered the room just out of the webcam's focus. Howard's face dropped, his eyes going wide as they moved closer, their images becoming clear. 'Run William, get out now, run.'

Before he had a chance to move, the centre figure raised his silenced Glock in his gloved hand and squeezed off two shots, one in the back of William's head, the other in the centre of his back. The bullet exited through William's chest, spraying the webcam in blood, leaving Howard staring at a red-tinted image of the men in balaclavas.

'Let me assure you, gentlemen, there is not a place on this Earth I won't find you and your boss,' Howard said, his voice calm but deadly serious.

From his hotel room in The Metropol in Moscow, Howard's last view of the control room was a levelled gun and a flash as the webcam was shot apart.

'Jesus, did you hear that guy?' said one of the masked invaders.

'Zip it, and wipe all the hard drives and backup servers. The boss wants the audio files of his conversations deleted,' said the gunman, pushing William's slumped body off his chair and onto the floor. He took William's place and started tapping furiously over the keyboard.

'Get a move on, we've gotta be out of here in five minutes,' he said, placing a little plastic box on the desk beside him.

CHAPTER 28

Terence Crawford shook hands and smiled politely as he left the meeting. Walking down the steps, his insides were doing somersaults. He nervously checked his phone for messages as he headed towards his parked car.

Why haven't I been alerted about officers down? It should have happened by now. Damn you, James for getting me involved in your shit storm.

He pressed the unlock button on the car key as he approached. The indicators flashed to the sound of a double pip as the doors clicked unlocked. Sliding into the driver's seat, Terence clicked on his seat belt and put the key in the ignition. He was about to turn it when a low chuckle made him jump. He spun around as the chuckle turned into a manic laugh. A bearded Middle Eastern man with long hair stared back at him from the back seat with spaced-out, dilated pupils. Terence's eyes went wide at the recognition of the suicide vest the young man was wearing. Its pouches were filled with explosive that daisy-chained with wires from pocket to pocket. As the laughter turned to incoherent mumblings, Terence's eyes flicked to the man's hands, looking in panic for the usual depressed trigger in the man's hand. Shocked and confused when he saw none, Terence reached for the door release in blind panic. The ringing of a mobile in the man's vest, followed by a blinding light, stopped him from ever getting out. Terence never heard the explosion that shattered the windows of the adjacent office block. The man, Terence, and the car were destroyed in a massive fireball. Fifty metres down the road, a man hung up his mobile, turned the ignition of his BMW, and drove smoothly off, away from the wailing car alarms and screaming bystanders.

———

Across London, James Bullman had gone for a mid-morning walk. He passed Westminster Abbey heading towards the river, and slowed as he passed the Houses of Parliament, pretending to look up at the scaffold-covered Big Ben. He knew he was being followed; he'd known since he left his house that morning. Resuming his walk, he crossed the road and ducked into Caffè Nero to get a coffee. He ordered a latte and waited patiently as the coffee machine bubbled and steamed loudly. Taking it to the little utility table with a bin, sugar and stirrers, James stood next to another customer as he ripped the top of the little sugar packets and tipped them into his drink. The customer next to him put the lid on his coffee and turned close behind James.

'Mission accomplished,' he said in a low voice before heading out the door. James's mouth curled into a smile as he popped the lid on his coffee and exited the shop. Noting his tail from the corner of his eye, he headed to the embankment and took a leisurely stroll along the Thames before heading back to his office.

CHAPTER 29

On the outskirts of Moscow, the Mercedes 4x4 drove silently into the Perovo district. Some kids on bikes followed it with their eyes as it passed, trying to see through the blacked-out glass at the occupants. They bumped down the kerb and cycled away from a wheel-less car jacked up on breeze blocks. Peddling as fast as they could, they cut across the neglected, rusty playground in the middle of the complex, using the shortcut to catch the car up as it drove around the estate. It pulled up outside a ten-storey apartment block and sat there, the engine ticking over with twin steam trails floating out of the exhausts. The kids sped towards it, skidding their bikes to the side as they stopped on the kerb opposite. They stared with tough little faces as the engine stopped and the door opened. The car rocked as the formidable Pasha got out, giving them a sideways warning look.

'Hey mister, nice car. Give us 2000 rubles and we'll make sure nothing happens to it,' the eldest boy yelled, while the others did their best to look menacing.

'Fuck off, little boys,' growled Pasha, pulling his jacket

to one side to show the Desert Eagle .50 sitting in his shoulder holster.

'Pasha, wait,' said Annika, sliding stylishly out of the rear of the car in a navy blue trouser suit. She stared at the boys with cold, ice-blue eyes. 'You, boy, what is your name?'

'Who wants to know?' the eldest boy said, his chin up as he held her stare with defiant confidence.

The younger boys in the gang edged back, torn between their loyalty to the eldest and shitting themselves and legging it.

'Annika Volkov, that's who,' she replied, walking across the road towards him, the heels of her Christian Louboutin's tapping on the tarmac.

The boy's confidence faltered. She could see the fear creeping in behind his defiant look.

'Come, boy, tell me your name or I'll get Pasha here to beat it out of you,' she said, no hint of emotion in her voice.

'Sorry, it's Adrian, Miss Volkov,' he said, his voice a little shaky.

'How old are you, Adrian?'

'Fourteen, miss,' he said as she stood inches away, her expensive perfume washing over him.

She opened her purse and pulled out a large clip of money. She peeled off a couple of 5000 ruble notes and flicked them towards Adrian between her fingers.

'Look after the car, Adrian,' she said, the faintest hint of a smile flicking across her face before she turned and clicked her way into the apartment block. Pasha stared at the boys before spitting on the floor and turning slowly to follow Annika inside. She walked down the corridor, her body moving with all the grace of a catwalk model. Spinning on her heels at apartment 23, she stepped to one side and stood motionless for Pasha to hammer his heavy fist on the apartment door.

'Ok, ok, I'm coming, don't knock the door off its hin —' Alek Lebedev's face fell as he opened the door and found the space filled by an angry-looking Pasha. 'Er, Pasha, what can I do for you?' said Alek, backing into the tiny apartment to avoid Pasha as he walked straight at him.

Entering the living room, Pasha moved to one side. Annika's petite frame came into view, her menacing presence making her seem ten feet tall.

'Mr Lebedev, did I not make my instructions clear regarding Mr Pearson's fate?' she said, her ice-blue eyes boring into him.

'Yes, yes you did, but Pearson is proving to be harder to deal with than anticipated. I—'

Pasha moved forward drawing the large Desert Eagle handgun out of its holster. He pressed the barrel to Alek's forehead.

'I do not pay you for problems. I pay you to make the lives of the people I put in your prison a living hell, and right now, Mr Pearson is that person. Now, if you cannot do this little thing I ask, you are of no use to me,' Annika said, her face without emotion, her cold eyes without forgiveness.

'I—I—I will,' stammered Alek, his eyes wide and mind in panic.

'Shoot him, Pasha.'

'No, no, no, he will suffer, I promise, please don't,' Alek shrieked, his teary eyes locked on Pasha's tensing trigger finger.

The gun made a loud click as the hammer hit an empty chamber. Alek's legs turned to jelly. He lost control of his bladder as he fell to the floor, a dark patch spreading around his crotch.

'Make Mr Pearson suffer, Mr Lebedev, or next time there will be a bullet in the chamber,' Annika said, spinning on her heels and heading out of the apartment.

Pasha looked at Alek in disgust. Just to enforce Annika's words, he pulled the slide back and chambered a round before turning deliberately slowly and following Annika out of the apartment. When they exited the block, Adrian and his gang of kids stood around the car, proudly guarding it.

'How would you like to make more money than you can dream of, Adrian?' Annika said to him as Pasha opened the back door of the car for her.

'Yes, Miss Volkov, I'll do anything,' Adrian said, without a second thought.

'Good. You and your boys work for me now. One of my men will be here tomorrow morning. He will give you a phone. We call, you answer. Any time, day or night, you answer, ok? You and your boys deliver packages and do errands for me. You do good, you get money. You let me down, you answer to Pasha,' Annika said, holding her intense gaze to enforce her words.

'Yes, Miss Volkov, thank you. Tomorrow we will be here, thank you.'

Annika gave a small nod, then slid into the back of the car. Pasha closed the door and snarled at the boys. 'Now fuck off,' he growled.

They didn't need telling twice. Spinning their bicycles around, they peddled off across the run-down playground.

Pasha smiled to himself once they had gone. He walked around the car and got into the driving seat.

'Where to?' he asked over his shoulder.

'Cafe Pushkin, I'm meeting an old friend for lunch.'

Clicking the ignition, Pasha moved the powerful car smoothly away.

CHAPTER 30

Howard exited the lift and walked through the hotel foyer. His face was serious as he walked.

'Lem,' said Howard, as he passed the man sitting on the reception sofa, his head hidden behind a paper.

Flicking the paper down, Lem frowned at Howard's sombre greeting. He got up and followed Howard to the seating area at the far end of the bar.

'Large scotch on the rocks,' Howard said to the same pretty, young waitress.

'Vodka on ice,' said Lem, waiting until she moved away before addressing him. 'I see trouble in your face, my friend.'

'Yes, I'm afraid I have to return to London later tonight,' said Howard, managing a smile when the waitress returned with the drinks.

'Must be quite serious to drag you away,' said Lem, the habit of being in intelligence making him fish for answers.

'It is, and it's linked to Annika Volkov and Daniel's abduction. I just don't know how yet.'

There was a pause of awkward silence until Lem finally spoke. 'Mmm, serious indeed. I have some news on your man.'

'Is he still alive?' Howard said, looking Lem straight in eye, his face expressionless but his voice sombre.

'I believe so. My contacts tell me the police are saying your man picked up in the Kapotnya district is Dank Kaslov, a convicted murderer who has been on the run for the last six months. He's been taken to Lefortovo Prison,' said Lem, taking a big swig of his vodka.

'Can you get him out?'

'It's tricky. Someone has gone to a great deal of trouble to get him in there. They have changed all Kaslov's identification, fingerprints, blood type and dental records to match your man. If I get involved questions will be asked. If it came out that five years ago I did a deal with you for this man to kill the Volkovs, well, let's just say your friend won't be the only one thrown in Lefortovo Prison.'

'I'm sorry, Lem, I've inconvenienced you enough,' said Howard, his mood sinking even lower.

'Now, now, my friend, I didn't say I wouldn't help you. I just said it's tricky,' said Lem, a wide grin spreading across his face.

'Go on,' said Howard, his interest suddenly piqued.

'I have a contact who can help you get word to your man.'

'And why would he help us?' said Howard.

'Because the Volkovs killed many of his family and put his son in Lefortovo Prison. You could leave your little entourage here while you return to London, and I will arrange a meet.'

'Yes, I could,' said Howard, not surprised that Lem had checked if he was here alone.

'Excellent, now cheer up, my friend, let us have another

drink,' said Lem, putting his hand up and clicking his fingers for the waitress.

'And what is this contact's name?'

'Kristof Turgenev, he's Russian Mafia, but he will help you. Annika Volkov shot him in his car then set light to him, leaving him for dead,' said Lem, downing the rest of his vodka as the waitress brought their order.

'Thank you,' said Howard in perfect Russian to the waitress.

'You're welcome, sir,' she replied with a pleasant smile.

'And the meet?'

'Have your men out front in one hour. I will have them picked up and taken to him,' said Lem, raising a toast to Howard. 'Nostrovia.'

'Nostrovia,' Howard said, returning the toast.

CHAPTER 31

Sitting in the communal area outside their cell, Danny, Leonid and Valerik spotted Filip moving hastily towards them. He sat beside them and looked nervously around for guards before fast-talking in Russian.

'What's he saying?' said Danny.

'English, Filip, English,' said Valerik, nodding his head towards Danny.

'Er, sorry. I got it, I got the map.'

'Shh,' said Leonid, as all four men's eyes worked up and down the long, three-storey corridor that doubled as a communal area.

There was a guard at the top end and one above them on the third-floor gangway that ran along the outside of the cells. They waited patiently until he moved away, their eyes willing him to keep on going. When he did, they turned their attention back to Filip.

'Show us,' said Valerik.

Filip pulled out a wedge of folded paper. He unfolded one and passed it over. Danny looked across to see part of a hand-drawn, detailed map of the prison with rooms, gates and locked doors all marked in pencil.

'Where did you get it?' said Danny.

'There's an old guy on D-Wing, he's been here for years. Knows the place back to front. It's on four pieces of notepaper as it's all he had, but it's good,' said Filip, grinning.

'You did good, Filip,' said Leonid.

'Warden's coming,' said Danny, eyeing Alek Lebedev making a beeline for them.

'Take the map and go,' Leonid said to Filip.

Shoving the map into his trouser pocket, Filip scooted away with his back to the approaching warden.

'You three, laundry duty,' Lebedev shouted, whacking his baton down onto the bolted-down metal table top for added effect.

When none of the three men so much as blinked, Lebedev's face flushed with a mixture of anger and frustration.

'Come, laundry duty,' Valerik said to Danny in English, as he and Leonid rose slowly, eyeing Lebedev with contempt.

They followed Lebedev to the barred gate at the top of the cell block and waited as he unlocked it, pushed it open and ushered them through, clanging the gate shut behind them.

As passed through several more locked gates, Leonid couldn't help walking closely behind Lebedev, sizing himself up for height and build. Happy with the match, he turned his head and winked at Danny.

They came to a door with a guard outside. He gave Lebedev a look and a nod that Danny didn't like, all nervous, eyes flicking from Lebedev to them. He unlocked the door and pulled it open for them to follow Lebedev inside. The room was large, with a row of industrial dryers rumbling around down one side and a row of large washing machines along the other wall. Five inmates moved around the centre, working on steam presses before folding and loading prison uniforms, bedding sheets and blankets into steel cages with wheels on the bottom. Danny recognised three of them as V members. By the snarls and tensing body language from Leonid and Valerik, they'd noticed them too.

Lebedev pointed his baton at each of them in turn, flicking it and pointing to a steam press and a pile of waiting laundry for each of them. He walked over to a guard at the far end of the room and spoke quietly in his ear before leaving the laundry. The hairs on the back of Danny's neck stood up at the same nervous look he'd seen on the guard as they entered. With his senses on alert, Danny started the repetitive task of pressing sheets and loading the cages.

They worked on for twenty minutes, the tension never leaving the room as the guard and other inmates continued to flick fleeting glances in their direction. Looking over as a blast of hot air hit him, Danny watched two inmates he didn't recognise open the large dryer door beside him. The guard walked over to them as they pulled the heavy linen out into a laundry cart. He said something in their ears then left the laundry while they followed him. This left the three of Volkov's gang members hovering around a linen cart, their body language tense.

'Be ready, something's going down,' Danny said, leaning across to Leonid on the steam press in front of him.

Leonid repeated the message to Valerik as Danny turned towards the entrance door. His fears were confirmed: the door had been left open and the guard had disappeared.

'Fuckers.'

Danny turned back to the source of Valerik's growl. Three V's had pulled metal bars and a carving knife from underneath the blankets in their laundry cart. Instinctively, Danny swung his head back to the door, just in time to see Sarkis Kiselyov and two of his men entering the laundry, metal bars in their hands, and a fish knife in Sarkis's. Without a second thought, Danny grabbed a blanket and spun it around his forearm to make thick, padded protection. Diving back into the laundry cart, Danny pulled a bedsheet out and twisted it around into a rope. Wrapping the ends around each wrist, he snapped it tight. Behind Danny, Valerik and Leonid grabbed a linen cage and charged at the men at the back of the room, gritted teeth and the fury of men who'd grown up in gangland Moscow written on their faces.

Leaving them to it, Danny turned away from the crash and rattle as Valerik hit two of the men with the cage, his attention focused on Sarkis and his two men as they fanned out to attack him from all sides. They faltered for a second, unnerved by Danny standing perfectly still, his knees slightly bent, arms out in front of him, knuckles white as he gripped the improvised rope between them.

With his face as hard as granite, Danny's dark, hawk-like eyes fixed on Sarkis in the centre, while his brain kept a check on the two men in his peripheral vision as they closed in from either side. The guy on the left broke first, charging Danny with the heavy iron bar raised above his head. Pivoting, Danny raised his forearm with the blanket wrapped around it. As the iron bar struck from above, Danny's leg was already moving, kicking the guy in the balls with such force his feet left the ground. Sensing the guy on the right, Danny spun around, snapping his head back and wrists apart as the man powered the metal bar down to where his head had been a split second earlier. With his power already committed to the strike, the guy's arm came down onto the improvised rope between Danny's hands. Spinning the rope around, Danny trapped one wrist before spinning around the other. With the guy's arms locked in the rope, Danny yanked him forward, head-butting him on the bridge of the nose as he came close. Spinning him loose, the dazed man sat back on the lip of a giant dryer, grabbing the open door to steady himself.

Catching a flash of steel out of the corner of his eye, Danny recoiled just in time to see the fish knife pass in front of his eyes. Jumping backwards, Danny kicked out, knocking the dazed, headbutted guy through the opening and into the dryer. Slamming the door shut behind him, Danny punched the ON button to muffled screams and tumbling thuds. Sarkis shouted and swore at his other man as he shook his head and inched towards the exit, breathing heavily as he held his crotch.

Sarkis bent down and picked up the dropped iron bar with his free hand. Unwrapping the sheet from his wrists, Danny chucked it on the floor and picked up the iron bar from the man in the dryer. As Danny and Sarkis circled each other around the steam press, he glanced at the far end of the room. One of the Sarkis's men was trying to crawl towards the exit, while Valerik knocked seven bells out of his mate. The third guy ran away from Leonid, picking his crawling mate up as he went. Taking advantage of Danny's glance, Sarkis took a stab at Danny across the steam press. The razor-sharp fish knife tore through his top, its tip sinking into the soft flesh of Danny's side. Before the blade got any deeper, Danny whacked the back of Sarkis's hand with the metal bar, breaking bones and causing him to drop the knife.

Quick as a flash, Danny reached forward and grabbed

Sarkis's hair, pulling his head down onto the flat surface before ramming the lid of the steam press down onto his face. Holding him there with all his body weight, Sarkis let out an agonising scream as the red-hot steam blistered his flesh. Danny eventually released the press, letting Sarkis fall back out. He grabbed his blistered, peeling face with shaking hands before getting to his feet and scrabbling out the door.

'Let him go, Valerik. His death would be hard to explain. Tell him to take his friend with him,' said Danny, opening the dryer to let the guy out.

He fell on the floor gasping for breath, his hands blistered from trying to hold himself off dryer's hot drum. He tried to stand up and failed, puking on the floor, his mind still scrambled from rolling over and over. Limping over, the guy Valerik had been beating helped him up and shuffled to the exit, watching Danny cautiously with the eye that wasn't swollen shut.

'Hey, you 're bleeding,' said Leonid, looking concerned.

'It's ok, it's just a flesh wound. It looks worse than it is,' said Danny, taking his shirt off.

He picked up the bedsheet and wrapped it around his middle, then grabbed a new prison shirt out of a metal cage and put it on over the top.

'Bunch of pussies, huh,' Valerik said, his usual grin returning to his face.

'Quick, we've gotta clean this place up,' Danny said.

A few minutes later, Alek Lebedev came charging in with three other guards, batons raised, expecting to see Danny and the others rolling around in agony on the floor. He stopped dead at the sight of the three men calmly steaming and folding sheets before loading the cages. A flash of fear crossed his whitening face before anger took its place. It was only there for a second, but Danny caught it.

He's in shit because he's fucked it up again.

'You three, back to your cells,' he yelled in Russian.

Danny stood defiantly, glaring at Lebedev as he walked over and put his face inches from Danny's.

'Back to cell, dead man,' he said in broken English.

CHAPTER 32

Well this is a crock of shit, Danny's in a maxium security prison, the boss has fucked off back to London because some wanker broke into HQ and killed William, and we're standing here like a couple of pricks waiting to be picked up by the Moscow Mafia,' grumbled John as he and Tom stood out the front of the Hotel Metropol waiting for their contact.

'That's what we signed up for, Jonny boy,' Tom muttered back.

'Not me, mate, I thought it would be all fast cars and loose women,' John replied, managing a chuckle.

'We've had fast cars.'

'Yeah, but there's usually some guy hanging out of its window shooting at us. Hang on, heads up,' said John, nodding towards a blacked-out Range Rover pulling up outside the hotel.

'Why's it always a Range Rover with these guys?' said Tom as the front window slid down.

'Hey, James Bond guys, get in the back, yeah? We take you to Kristof,' said the driver in broken English, his dark shades sitting slightly crooked on his flat, broken nose, a gold tooth glinting in the sunlight as he beamed widely.

'Here we go,' muttered Tom.

They shared a look, then opened the back door of the car and climbed in. The second the door shut they were thrown back in their seats as the car accelerated away. A carbon copy of the driver, without the broken nose, swung around in the passenger seat to look at them, a large Magnum handgun in hand.

'Welcome to Moscow, secret agent men. I'm Pyotr. The boss is dying to meet you and this man who killed the Volkovs,' said Pyotr, grinning and waving the gun around in his hand as if he'd forgotten he was holding it.

Tom just nodded his acknowledgement to Pyotr as he tried to keep an eye on where they were going. They turned out of a side road to pass the colourful St Basil's Cathedral by Red Square, it's bright, candy-coloured, twirling domes glistening in the sunlight. From there they crossed the Moskva River before zigzagging through side streets and finally pulling up outside an unremarkable bar. Pyotr got out first, still making no effort to conceal his gun. He opened the back door and beckoned Tom and John to follow him inside. He led them through the bar and out the back without the bar staff and customers batting an eyelid.

'Is safe. Family. We are all family here,' Pyotr said when he noticed Tom looking.

They continued up a narrow staircase and onto a landing. Pyotr paused outside a door and knocked.

'Come in,' came a reply in Russian.

When the door opened, Tom could see a silver-haired old guy with a burn scar up one side of his face that ended in the middle of his crew cut, just above his missing ear. His face was lined and hard as stone, but his dark blue eyes burned youthfully as he rose from his seat.

'Come, sit, sit, you are welcome. Pyotr, go get drink and food, da,' he said, waving Pyotr off as he sat back down. 'I am Kristof Turgenev. I must apologise about the meagre surroundings. When your friend killed the Volkovs five years ago we took over and ran the city. That was until Annika Volkov came of age. She did a deal with the other families and drove us out, killing many of us and paying her contacts in the police and justice department to have my son Valerik and nephew Leonid put into Lefortovo Prison to suffer an eternity at the hands of her men. They think I'm dead, which is why we meet here, in safe place,' Kristof said pointing to his scarred face.

'And Danny's definitely in Lefortovo Prison?' asked Tom.

'Lem says he is, they have him as wanted murderer, Dank Kaslov.'

'And you can get word to him?'

'Da. I've, er, persuaded a guard to get a phone to Valerik. He will find your man,' said Kristof with a smile. He turned and patted a dog lying beside him. 'Don't worry, boy, you'll be back with your owner soon.'

The door opened and Pyotr entered with a tray of glasses and ice and a bottle of vodka. Two women followed in behind him with pelmeni dumplings and a bowl of sour cream, and pirozhki puff pastries filled with meat and cheese.

'Sit, Pyotr,' said Kristof, filling the glasses with a generous helping of vodka. 'Drink. To new friends,' he said raising his glass. 'Nostrovia.'

'Nostrovia,' they all said in return.

'Now eat, eat,' said Kristof, slapping Tom on the shoulder.

An hour and substantial amount of vodka later, Pyotr

took them back to the car and drove them to the Hotel Metropol.

'We will call you as soon as we have news, ok,' Pyotr said, as they got out.

'Thank you, Pyotr,' said Tom.

'You're welcome. Goodbye, Mr Bond,' said Pyotr with a big grin.

The car raced off, leaving Tom and John standing in the same spot they'd been in a couple of hours earlier, only this time feeling a bit worse for wear.

'Fuck me, what just happened? My head's spinning,' said John.

'What shall we do now?' said Tom, walking towards the hotel as the doorman pulled the entrance door open for them.

'You want another drink?' smiled John.

'Er, ok.'

CHAPTER 33

Coming out of passport control at Heathrow's terminal 2, the fast clicking of his suitcase wheels on the terminal building's floor reflected Howard's eagerness to get out of the exit doors. He looked left to see his driver, Frank, standing next to his Audi Q7 in the drop off bay. Two police officers walked away from him, put out at being overruled by Frank's national security identification when they'd tried to move him on.

'Good flight, sir?' Frank said, opening the back door for Howard.

'Unfortunately, I fail to find the good in anything that's occurred over the last few days. HQ, Frank, quick as you like, please.' Howard said, devoid of his usual jovial demeanour.

'Certainly, sir,' Frank replied, shutting the door before walking round to the driver's side.

It took an hour to get to HQ as late afternoon drew into the capital's rush hour crawl. Frank finally pulled in alongside the unassuming building.

'Go home, Frank, I'm going to be here a while.'

'Very good, sir,' Frank replied. He waited until his boss had looked up to the camera and been buzzed into the building before he pulled away into the crawling traffic.

All eyes turned to look at Howard as he entered the office, pained looks at the loss of a team member and a visible awkwardness of not knowing what to say. Above the emotion, an ever-professional Edward Jenkins approached him and extended his hand in greeting.

'Sorry about your man.'

'Thank you, Edward, and thank you for stepping in with your forensic team,' said Howard, looking at William's workstation, clean and sterile with its replaced computer, chair and blood-stained carpet tiles, no sign left of the man who'd lost his life.

'It's no problem, although we haven't got much to go on. No prints, standard 9mm bullet and they left the building on foot, presumably cutting through to Cannock Street where there's no CCTV coverage. They did leave these though,' said Edward, picking up the little plastic box and handing it to Howard.

Howard opened the lid, his face creasing in an uncommon display of anger at the sight of the three audio bugs from Bullman's office. It only lasted a few seconds before Howard flipped back into calm control once more.

'Martin, be a good fellow and organise coffee for everyone, the usual for Edward and I,' he said with a smile.

'Yes, boss,' said Martin, heading around the room to take everyone's orders.

'Run me through what we do know,' Howard said, turning back to Edward.

'We know our Minister of Defence is behind the abduction of Daniel, although I'm still at a loss what his connection to Annika Volkov is. It can't be money;

Bullman inherited millions from his family estate when his parents died, and his salary is over £150,000 a year.'

'Mmm, I'll keep digging. Go back to Victor and Yuri Volkov. Perhaps there's a link there somewhere. What about Terence Crawford and his little band of men?'

'The remains of the device that blew up the Chief's car would suggest a vest worn by the second man who has been identified as Malik Osman, a young Palestinian with extremist beliefs and a whole host of other documented mental issues.'

'How very convenient. I don't buy that for a minute. You suicide bomb an event or gathering, the place where a pre-planned or known event is going to happen. Not the back of a single man's car parked in an unplanned location. What about the armed response team?' Howard said, still twirling the little box of bugs around in his hands.

'They know how it works, ten minutes in and they were climbing all over each other to do a deal. Crawford personally selected each one of them before he was Chief. Their outstanding result rate was always accredited to him, which helped to accelerate his career to the top. It transpires that some of their arrests and drug busts are linked to payments and information from rival drug dealers wanting to cut out the competition. Crawford sent them to get Daniel and told them to give him to two Russian guys in the stolen police riot van. We found the van this morning, it's been crushed into a cube at a scrap yard in Slough,' said Edward, taking one of the coffees from Martin as he returned.

'Thank you, Martin,' Howard said, taking the other. 'Any joy with Bullman's other phone?'

'Er, yes and no. We got a number and list of calls from the service provider. He's clever though, never texts and the voicemail is turned off, so we couldn't get anything on those. The phone went dead the day you bugged his office, hasn't been on since.'

'Thank you, Edward. I know this isn't really your remit, but I appreciated yours and MI6's help,' Howard said, pausing to take a gulp of coffee before walking to the front of the room to address his team. 'Right, listen up, people, we are all saddened by the loss of our friend and colleague, William. What has happened here is an outrage. Rest assured, with your help, I intend to find the perpetrators and hold them to account for his murder. Let's get to work.'

The hushed quiet changed into a hum of activity as people got back to their computers and talked on phones.

'Brian,' Howard said, wandering over to his desk

'Yes, boss,'

'Go back five or six years and get everything we have on Victor and Yuri Volkov, and any link you can find between them and James Bullman.'

'On it, boss.'

'Martin.'

'Yes, boss,'

'Bullman's ditched the burner phone. See Edward and get the list of numbers he has from the service provider for incoming and outgoing calls. Check them all out for me, please.'

'Ok,' Martin said, turning towards Edward.

'Oh, and do a triangulation on Bullman's office and home address, all providers. See if we get any phone activity other than his known mobile in those two locations. If he's got a new burner phone, I want to know,' said Howard, his mind in full operation mode as he paced up and down.

'Lionel,' he said, moving swiftly over to his desk.

'Yep.'

'Get me a list of all the known assets used by us and the MoD, specifically ones commissioned by Bullman that are in the UK and could have been in London at the time of William's murder.'

'Yes, boss.'

'Any news of Daniel?' Edward said, finishing his coffee and picking his jacket off the back of a chair.

'Er, yes. He's inside a Moscow prison. Annika Volkov has a lot of influence in Moscow. She has him under the false ID of a Russian murderer.'

'Well, at least he's alive,' Edward said.

'Yes, for the moment. I have Tom and John still out there trying to get word to him.'

'Any idea how you're going to get him out?'

'None whatsoever, but knowing Daniel the answer will present itself sooner rather than later.'

'Let's hope so. I have to get back to the office now.'

'Yes, of course, you go, and thank you again, Edward,' Howard said, shaking Edward's hand before he turned and left.

'Right, gentlemen, let's get some results,' he said, turning back to his team.

CHAPTER 34

I n the MoD building in Whitehall, The Minister of Defence sat in his freshly swept, bug-free office. He was going through the daily routine chores, checking government contracts, changes in foreign policy and upgraded or downgraded threats to the country, when the phone rang.

'James Bullman,' he said gruffly.

'It's Larry Whistle, sir.'

'Yes, Larry, what have you got for me?' said James, his tone softening a little.

'Your man has returned from Moscow, sir, I have the audio stream uploaded on your secure portal.'

'Thank you, Larry. Remember, this is a category one situation. No one must know of this,' said James.

'Of course, sir,' said Larry, agreeing quickly.

'Good, good, and Larry, that promotion you've been after, do well on this and it's yours.'

'Eh yes, sir, thank you, sir,' Larry said excitedly, while James rolled his eyes and put the phone down.

He opened his laptop and logged into the secure portal.

Larry had already gone from his mind as he plugged in some headphones and hit play on the audio file. Sitting back in his chair, he listened to Howard's arrival at HQ as Edward Jenkins greeted him.

Dare to bug my office, would you? Well two can play that game, Howard.

He sat listening, frowning when Howard declared that he knew who was behind the abduction of Daniel Pearson.

You may know, old boy, but you'll never find the proof to air that view, or connect me with Annika Volkov.

Continuing to listen, he smiled to himself as they discussed the suicide bombing of Police Chief Superintendent Terence Crawford.

Buy it, don't buy it, I don't care, Howard, you've got nothing.

When he heard the part about them triangulating mobile signals to find his new phone, James pulled it out of his pocket, popped the sim out and snapped it, before twisting the cheap mobile in two. He pulled a Jiffy bag out of his desk and popped the pieces of the phone and sim into it; he'd dispose of it on the way home. When Howard and Edward moved onto the subject of tracking the assets who had breached the HQ and killed William, his face grew dark.

Now that could cause a problem. I may have to deal with that.

Finishing the recording, James logged out of the secure portal and shut the laptop down. Opening his briefcase, he placed the laptop and the Jiffy bag inside before leaving the office.

CHAPTER 35

'Hey, Ramon, how long have you got left, man?' said Valerik, lying on his bunk looking up at the bottom of his cell mate's bunk above him.

'Eleven weeks, three days and seven hours, not like I'm counting or anything,' said Ramon from above.

'It will go soon go, my friend. What you going to do when you get out?'

'Get as far away from this rotten city as possible,' came Ramon's blunt reply.

'Where will you g—'

Both men went silent, popping their heads up at the sound of the cell door being unlocked and opened. One of the guards, Taavi Putin entered. He looked unusually nervous as his eyes flicked from Ramon to Valerik.

'You, get out and wait in the corridor, now,' he said, pointing his baton at Ramon to emphasise his command.

As Ramon hopped down, Valerik swung his legs off the bed and sat tense, waiting for the beating he assumed would come. As soon as Ramon was outside, Taavi swung the cell door shut, cutting off Ramon's apologetic look of helplessness at not being able to help his friend. Valerik stared at Taavi defiantly as he moved towards him. To his surprise, instead of striking him with his baton, he reached into his pocket and pulled out something wrapped in a plastic bag and threw it in his lap. Valerik opened it to see a basic mobile phone with two spare batteries.

'You tell your father I've done what he asked. You leave my wife alone, and I want my dog back. Unhurt, you hear me?' said Taavi, his voice cracking as he spoke and tears welling up in his eyes. He wiped them dry on his sleeve, pulled the door open, and left, ignoring Ramon as he passed him.

'Fuck, I thought you were for it then, what the fuck was up with him?' Ramon said, stopping dead in his tracks at the sight of Valerik powering up the mobile phone.

'Hey, Ramon, keep an eye out for guards,'

'Ok,' said Ramon, giving him a nod as he leaned on the door frame, scanning the long cell block and its three floors above.

Valerik pressed the call button by the number stored in the phone. It seemed to take an excruciatingly long time to connect and start ringing.

'Valerik, is that you?'

'Papa, yes it's me,' said Valerik, the emotion getting to him despite his hard man image.

'How are you, son, those bastards haven't hurt you?'

'No, Papa, I'm ok, is good to talk to you.'

'You too. I have something I need you to do,' said Kristof.

'Anything, Papa, what do you need?' said Valerik, his eyes fixed on Ramon in case he had to get off and hide the phone quick.

'I need you to find somebody in there, an English man. They have him in as Dank Kaslov. His real name is Daniel

Pearson. This man is important, Valerik. He is the man who killed Yuri and old man Sebastian Volkov.'

'I know him, Papa, he's in a cell with Leonid, but how do you know about him?'

'His friends from England are looking for him, government friends, secret agent shit. Their boss knows that crazy old KGB guy, Lem Vassiliev,' said Kristof, pleased to talk to his son again.

'Hey, Papa, we have a plan to get out of here, but I need your help.'

'Anything. Talk to me, Valerik,' Kristof said, his voice excited about the prospect of getting his son out.

'I need you to hijack a garbage truck.'

CHAPTER 36

Sweating nervously as he drove into the Perovo district towards his apartment block, Alek Lebedev's eyes flicked to the rear-view mirror to see if he was being followed. He breathed a sigh of relief at the empty road behind him and not Annika Volkov's Mercedes 4x4 with the blacked-out windows hanging off his rear bumper.

Damn that fucking idiot Sarkis and his men. Why couldn't they just take care of that bloody Englishman. Annika will blame me for this.

A group of boys flew out of the rundown park in front of him, forcing his attention back to the road and causing him to brake sharply as they hopped their bicycles onto the kerb opposite, slid them to a halt and stared at him menacingly.

Fucking little bastards, why aren't they in school? I've seen that one with the expensive leather jacket and flash new phone around here before. He's usually in rags. I wonder who he robbed to get the money for that?

He stopped at the end of the road to get a view of the

entrance to his apartment block. No sign of the Mercedes or Pasha waiting for him. Checking the rear-view mirror, it was still clear of cars, just a view of the boy with the jacket. He was on the phone while the others rode around him.

Ok, I'm just going to get some clothes and money and stay at my sister's for a while.

Driving forward to the entrance, Alek got out. He had a last look around as he locked the car. The boys had cycled back across the road and were whizzing about in the park opposite. The boy with the leather jacket had got off his bicycle and stood looking Alek's way, his phone glued to his ear. Slightly unnerved, Alek went inside and headed for his apartment. His fingers shook as he rattled the keys in the lock and opened the door. Once inside, he didn't hang about. Pulling a large holdall from under his bed, Alek moved from drawer to drawer selecting clothes he would need for a couple of weeks at his sister's. Zipping the holdall up, he glanced out the window, checking each end of the street for any signs of Annika's car. Relieved to see the coast was clear, he grabbed the bag and headed for the door. Pulling it open, he jumped back to find the boy with the leather jacket standing in his way.

'Fuck off, kid, I'm in a hurry,' Alek said, pushing past Adrian as he hurried for the exit.

'Hey, Alek,' the boy shouted, stopping him as he neared the exit. Surprised at his name being shouted, Alex turned to look back at the boy. 'Miss Volkov says you've let her down for the last time,' Adrian said, his eyes looking down the sights of a Glock 17 handgun at Alek.

'What? Hey, kid, no, wait, I can explain. Please don't shoot,' Alek stammered back, his eyes on stalks and his heart beating wildly in his chest.

Adrian squeezed the trigger, putting a hole in the middle of Alek's chest and knocking him off his feet. He lay flat on his back, blood spreading across his warden's uniform as he stared at the yellow ceiling light above him until it faded into black.

Adrian slid the gun back in his jacket and pulled the phone Annika had given him out of his pocket. He took a photo of Alek's body and sent it. As he walked out of the apartment and back to his gang of kids in the park, it buzzed with a reply.

You have done well, Adrian.

You are now a true member of the Volkov Mafia.

CHAPTER 37

Tom woke first. He sat up in bed and stayed there for a while, trying to clear the alcohol fog from his head. He was sharing a twin room with John, who was snoring loudly in the single bed next to him. His mobile vibrated on the bedside table, dancing around with every buzz.

'Hello.'

'Hey, James Bond, get your shit together. We've been in contact with your man,' came the upbeat voice of Kristof.

'Great, is he ok?'

'Da, he's good. Listen, I'm sending Pyotr to pick you up. We have a plan to get your friend and my son and nephew out. We talk when you get here,' said Kristof, hanging up before Tom could answer.

Tom lowered the phone, taking a second for Kristof's words to break through the hangover. When they did, he leaped out of bed and launched a pillow at John's head, stopping the snoring in a spluttering, rude awakening.

'What the fuck's going on,' John grumbled as he rubbed his eyes.

'Everything, mate. Kristof's just called. They've been in contact with Danny and are planning a breakout, he's sending Pyotr over to pick us up,' said Tom, heading for the bathroom.

'Great, I hope the bastard doesn't poison us with more of that bloody vodka,' said John, slapping his cheeks to wake up.

Twenty minutes later they were out the front of the hotel, having a déjà vu feeling as the blacked-out Range Rover pulled up beside them. The window went down and the same driver grinned at them, his dark shades sitting slightly crooked on his flat, broken nose, and his gold tooth still glinting in the sunlight.

'Come on, tough guys, get in, get in,' he said, waving them over. They got in the back of the car, which, as the day before, pulled away the second the door clicked shut.

'Hey, guys, is a good day, da. Kristof is waiting for us. You will need these,' said Pyotr, passing a couple of bala-clavas back to them.

'Hey, Pyotr, what the fuck is going on?' said Tom holding the balaclava up.

'Is no big thing, English. We steal a garbage truck, that is all. Kristof will explain all,' said Pyotr, finding their puzzled looks highly amusing.

They drove for around twenty minutes to an industrial estate on the outskirts of the city before pulling in. Thirty metres up the road, a BMW X7 flashed its lights twice. The driver returned the signal, then pulled his balaclava down over his head.

'Come, put them on,' said Pyotr, pulling his down and drawing his Magnum from his jacket.

Tom looked at John, shrugged, and pulled the bala-clava onto his head. 'Pyotr, what the fuck are we doing here?' he asked.

'I told you, we steal garbage truck, is needed for the breakout tomorrow. The depot is up there, truck will be along soon,' said Pyotr, pointing to a collection of large industrial buildings beyond a high wall at the end of the road.

As if on cue, a blue garbage truck emerged from the entrance gates. It turned and moved slowly towards them. The driver gave a flash to the BMW and started creeping forward. When the truck was fifty metres away, he hit the accelerator and hurtled them forwards before handbraking the car sideways across the road in front of the truck. The BMW did the same from behind, trapping the truck between the two vehicles.

The driver and Pyotr raced out of the car, waving their guns and shouting something in Russian at the terrified bin men. They climbed out of the cab and shuffled off the road to one side as Pyotr continued to shout at them. Two men in balaclavas got out of the back of the BMW, ran to the cab of the truck, climbed in and revved the truck as they crunched it in gear. Giving a final wave of his gun at the bin men, Pyotr and the driver got back in the car and reversed it at speed, spinning it around and throwing it in gear to drive back the way they'd come. The garbage truck and the BMW followed close behind.

'Ha, easy yeah?' said Pyotr, pleased with himself as he pulled the balaclava off.

'Yeah, congratulations, you've got yourself a garbage truck,' said Tom sarcastically as he removed his mask.

They drove on in convoy for a few more miles before turning into a large garage and parking out the front, next to the BMW. The garbage truck drove on through the high roller doors, disappearing inside the garage.

'Come, we go inside,' Pyotr said, getting out.

They followed him into the unit to see Kristof climbing

out of the truck's cab with his balaclava still in his hand. He grinned at them as he approached and embraced them both.

'You're wondering what the fuck's going on, yes? Come into the office, I will tell you,' Kristof said, waving them into the little cabin in the corner of the unit.

They followed Kristof inside. He took a seat behind the office desk, so Tom and John sat on a row of metal chairs meant for waiting customers.

'Your man is good. He's sharing a cell with my nephew, ok. They are going to escape tomorrow by hiding in the kitchen garbage bins. We turn up at the scheduled time, tip them into the back of the garbage truck and drive straight out of the prison. My son says he has a map of the prison. The garbage truck goes in through the main gates into the main courtyard. Once we're inside, the guards will open a second gate so we can reverse up to a courtyard at the back of the kitchens and the garbage bins,' Kristof said, the burn scar creasing as he grinned excitedly.

'How are they going to get from their cells to the bins?' said John.

'The guard we used for the phone drop will unlock the doors to the kitchen.'

'You've got his dog, right?' said Tom, remembering the dog from their last meeting.

'Haha, no, we gave the dog back, it kept pissing all over the place.'

'So how are you getting him to do it?'

'When we take dog back, we swap it for the wife. She does not piss everywhere,' said Kristof, breaking into a grin again.

'Ok, so why didn't we just hijack the truck on the way to the prison?' said Tom, puzzled.

'We have to, er, how you say, change, er, modify the

compactor plates so they won't get crushed when we empty the bins into the back. They will fall into the bucket with trash, and slide under the compactor into the empty storage area at front of the truck. We will stop real truck on the way to the prison and drive this one in instead. Is good plan, da?'

'Er, yeah, it sounds good to me. What time do we go?' said Tom, looking across at John, who nodded his affirmation.

'The garbage truck gets to the prison for 7:00 a.m. We leave here at six, stop real garbage truck and drive to prison.'

CHAPTER 38

'The boy killed Lebedev, then,' said Pasha, following Annika around the finished kitchen and into the huge lounge of the rebuilt Volkov estate.

'Yes, he will make a good foot soldier, loyal to me,' she replied without turning, her eyes fixed on the three men struggling to fit a huge hundred-inch TV to the wall.

'I didn't think the little shit had it in him,' replied Pasha, throwing one of the TV engineers a menacing look for daring to glance his way.

'Maybe I'm a better judge of character than you,' Annika said, turning to throw him a smug smile.

'Maybe we should ask Pearson about that,' grumbled Pasha in reply.

Annika spun around on her heels, her ice-blue eyes cutting into Pasha as her petite frame seemed to grow with her anger.

'As loyal as you have been to my family, do not overstep the mark, Pasha.'

'My apologies,' said Pasha sarcastically. He may have secretly wanted to dispose of Annika and take over, but she was a Volkov, and as such, was protected by some of the largest Mafia families in Russia. Killing Annika would sign his own death warrant.

The flash of anger on Annika's face went as quickly as it had arrived. She spun back on her heels and focused her attention on the men standing back from the newly mounted TV, wiping the sweat off their brows.

'It's too low. I want it five centimetres higher. Take it down and do it again,' she said, telling, not asking. 'Come, Pasha,' she said, blanking the men as she walked out of the room.

'Where are we going?'

'I have had enough of Mr Pearson and those Turgenev scum. The games are over. It is time to put them down like the dogs they are. We are going to the prison to see the governor. We will have them transferred to another prison.'

'What good will that do?'

'They will never arrive at their destination, Pasha. You will stop the transport and bring them here. Then I'm going to watch you torture them until I decide to kill them.'

'I'll bring the car around,' said Pasha smiling. Finally, he could do what he should have done long ago.

CHAPTER 39

Danny laid on his top bunk, staring in the moonlight at the peeling paint on the ceiling, the internal clock in his head telling him it was around 4:00 a.m. A few more hours until the guard, Taavi, unlocked the cell door and the gates to the kitchen. Valerik told him his father, Kristof, had Taavi's wife hostage to make him do as they asked. Danny wasn't a big fan of kidnap and extortion, but it was hard to take the moral high ground when you're stuck in a Russian prison.

"Keep to the plan, a simple plan. Simple plans work the best; less moving parts to go wrong. Get to the kitchen. Bury yourself in the food bins out back. 7:00 a.m. Kristof with Tom and John turn up in the garbage truck, chuck us in the back and drive out. Simple."

'Hey, Danny, you awake?' came Leonid's hushed voice from the bunk below.

'Yeah.'

'I can't sleep. What if they search the bin?'

'They won't. The bin tips into the garbage truck and the compactor crushes the rubbish, that's what should happen, that's what they'll think has happened. Unless your uncle doesn't stop the real garbage truck, then we'll be crushed to death,' said Danny, in a hushed reply.

'A cheery thought, thanks,' said Leonid, even more awake than he was a minute ago.

'Hey, he's your uncle, I've never met the guy.'

'Kristof is a great man. He says he will be here, he will be here.'

'Then there's nothing to worry about, is there?' said Danny.

The cell fell silent as both men lay lost in their thoughts.

———

'Hey, six o'clock, let's go, let's go,' shouted Kristof.

Dressed in blue overalls and high-visibility jackets, Tom and John climbed into the back seats of the cab. Kristof jumped into the driver's seat as Pyotr got into the passenger side.

'Hey, you ready, guys? Let's go get your friend, eh?' said Pyotr over the noise of the big diesel engine.

'Ok, let's go,' said Kristof to Tom and John before winding the window down and yelling at the others in Russian. They got into the Range Rover and BMW and pulled out of the garage in front of the truck, tearing off down the road before disappearing around the corner.

'Don't worry, they will stop the truck. We will catch up with them in a few minutes,' Kristof shouted to Tom and John in the back.

———

At six, Danny heard the echoing tap of footsteps, followed by the metallic clunk of the cell door being unlocked. As it swung open, the gaunt, sleepless face of Taavi Putin came into view. He stepped back without looking them in the eye to reveal Valerik standing behind him. As soon as Danny and Leonid leapt out of their bunks and moved out into the communal area, Taavi pulled their cell door shut and locked it. He walked ahead of them, heading nervously towards the gate at the end of the block. Leonid slapped Valerik on the back as the three men scooted after Taavi.

Taavi repeated the process, unlocking and locking the gates and doors as Danny and the other two moved through. Walking ahead a few paces as Taavi locked the gate behind them, Danny froze at the distant sound of keys rattling and a gate opening somewhere down a corridor to his left.

'Back, back, there's someone coming,' Danny whispered, pushing Valerik and Leonid back out of sight and into Taavi.

'Taavi, somebody's coming,' Leonid repeated in Russian.

'Eh, shit, fuck, in here,' Taavi said, his eyes wide in panic and his hands shaking as he rattled through his big bunch of keys, trying desperately to find the one to open the door beside them.

'Tell him to hurry up. If they come around that corner, I'm going to have to take them out before they raise the alarm,' Danny whispered to Leonid, the echoes of approaching footsteps growing ever closer.

Danny blanked the sound of Leonid ushering Taavi on in Russian. He stepped near the corner to the corridor and stood muscles tense, knees bent and fist drawn back, concentrating on the approaching footsteps as he tensed, storing all his energy ready for his one shot at a knockout punch.

Here they come, fifteen metres, twelve, ten.

A tap on his shoulder and movement behind him made Danny step silently backwards and hop through the open door. Taavi pushed the metal door closed excruciatingly slowly so it didn't boom with the usual noise they were used to hearing every morning, noon, and night. Instead, it made the faintest of clicks as the footsteps sounded outside, then stopped.

Seconds passed in silence. Danny could hear the blood rushing in his ears as his heart pounded. Taavi's face was pale, and he looked ready to have a heart attack. As Danny prepared to rush the door as it opened, the footsteps moved off, fading to silence until they heard the clang of a gate being unlocked further along. Breathing sighs of relief, they moved back out into the corridor and followed Taavi until they finally entered the kitchen. Taavi unlocked the door into the courtyard, throwing his hand up to stop the men as he checked the coast was clear.

'Ok, it is clear, go,' he said, stepping back.

Danny and Leonid went first, Taavi catching Valerik's arm as he passed.

'I did as you asked, yes. You will return my wife unharmed,' he said with a pleading look in his eyes.

'You did good, Taavi. Your wife will be fine. You have my word on it,' said Valerik, looking him in the eyes.

Taavi nodded and let him go, locking the door behind them and exiting the kitchen to get back to his rounds before his work colleagues noticed his absence. Out in the courtyard, Danny lifted the heavy lid on the big industrial bins. The stench of rotting food was overpowering.

'Shit, that fucking stinks,' said Valerik, putting his arm over his nose and mouth.

'There's not time to think about it. You two get in that one before anyone comes. Bury yourselves deep and sit tight. I'll shut the lid and get in this one,' Danny said, his eyes darting about the courtyard for guards.

'Ah, fuck,' said Valerik, swinging himself over the side, grimacing as he landed in between the garbage bags and some unidentifiable rotting food substance. Leonid jumped in the other side of the bin and the two men dug themselves down, gagging at the smell as they covered their heads.

'Right, no noise,' said Danny, lowering the lid. He moved to the other bin, took a last look around before throwing himself in over the side. He moved the bags and rotting trash around until he was up to his waist in it, then pulled the lid down and buried himself in the darkness.

Fuck it stinks. If I spend too long in here I'm going to fucking puke.

CHAPTER 40

'Hey, Kristof, is just like the old days, yeah,' said Pyotr, buzzing.

'Da, just like the old days.'

Kristof drove the garbage truck carefully for twenty minutes or so, keeping to the speed limits, junctions and traffic lights. He eventually turned down a quiet side road where the other garbage truck sat sandwiched between the BMW and Range Rover. Kristof lowered his window as he pulled alongside. One of his men handed him the paperwork from the real truck and nodded as Kristof grabbed it and passed it to Pyotr before driving on. As they passed, Tom could see Kristof's men pointing guns at the faces of the terrified garbage men through the open cab doors.

The smiles and banter dropped as they drove on towards the prison in tense silence. The prison wasn't hard to spot with its high brick wall and imposing three-storey cell blocks behind it. They turned onto the approach road, driving through open blue metal gates into a carpark outside the prison wall. Two huge red entrance doors lay straight ahead of them. Stopping in front of them, Kristof lowered his window to the two approaching guards. He handed the paperwork from the real garbage truck over with a casual smile and sat back while they checked it.

'Ok, open up,' the man said into his radio before handing the paperwork back to Kristof. 'Pull into the courtyard and step out of the truck.'

The huge red doors cracked and ticked as they opened slowly outwards. Kristof gave a small wave to the man and drove carefully through the tight opening, pulling into the space pointed out by a guard.

'Follow us and say nothing,' said Kristof quietly over his shoulder to Tom and John. He turned the ignition off, and they all climbed out of the truck and stood to one side. The guards did an unenthusiastic routine search for weapons, drugs or contraband in the cab, while Tom watched a prison transport van pull into the courtyard and park on the opposite side. The driver and passenger got out and opened the back, ready for prisoners to be loaded. They walked across to a metal door and waited to be buzzed in, laughing and joking with one of the guards before disappearing inside. Looking back as the guards came out of the truck, they copied Kristof and put their arms up while the guards patted them down for weapons or drugs.

'Ok, turn it around and reverse it through the gate over there. The bins are lined up by the kitchens,' the guard said, turning away from them and speaking into his radio.

As Kristof started the truck, the gate opened ahead of them. He turned the truck around and backed it carefully towards the commercial bins located in a smaller courtyard by the kitchens. The two prison guards followed protocol, escorting the truck on either side as it reversed. The tension and feeling of being trapped grew by the second inside the cab as they moved up to the bins.

'You two stay here. Pyotr and me will load the bins,' said Kristof, engaging the parking brake. Tom and John nodded at him as he and Pyotr climbed out of the cab.

———

Stifling a gagging cough, Danny lay in the stench, listening to the sound of the approaching garbage truck. He half expected the lid to fly open and the arms of guards to grab him at any minute. Instead, he felt the bin move and rumble across the concrete courtyard before bashing into the lifting arms of the garbage truck. A second later he heard the noise of the hydraulic pistons and felt the bin lifting into the air. Taking as deep a breath as he could without throwing up, Danny braced himself as the bin tilted upside down and he fell into the bucket at the back of the garbage truck under a waterfall of putrid garbage.

Remembering what Valerik had said, Danny lay flat and rolled towards the front of the truck, sliding under the modified compactor as it made all the right noises without compressing the garbage and him into a bloody mess. He sat in the darkness listening to the sound of the bin outside clattering back down. Moments later he heard the sound of the next bin clanging into the hydraulic lift, followed by the deafening sound of trash clattering into the rubbish bucket. Something soft rolled into Danny. He reached down into the darkness and grabbed the material of a prison top, pulling the body back out of the trash towards him. As Danny let go, a second body rolled towards him. A retching noise could be heard in the darkness as either Valerik or Leonid gagged on the stench.

'Quiet, hold it in,' whispered Valerik in the darkness.

They slid back until they could feel their shoulders touching the metal wall at the front of the garbage truck.

The noise of the hydraulics dropping the empty bin stopped, leaving just the sound of the ticking-over diesel engine, the tension in the back blocking out all thoughts of the stench they were sitting in. They held their breath at the sound of the bin rattling away, followed by the cab doors slamming shut and the big diesel engine revving as the truck pulled forward.

CHAPTER 41

'Good morning, I've got transfer papers for three prisoners, Valerik Turgenev, Dank Kaslov and Leonid Turgenev,' said the driver of the prison transport van handing his paperwork to the guard on the check-in desk.

He flicked through the pages, half-heartedly checking the names before reaching for the radio. 'Hey, Demi, can you and Oleg bring Valerik and Leonid Turgenev and Dank Kaslov here for prison transport?'

'On our way,' came Demi's crackly response over the radio.

———

'Come on, come on,' Kristof said under his breath, his eyes flicking from the guards standing either side of the cab to the gate as it opened excruciatingly slowly.

It finally opened fully. The two guards walked in front of the garbage truck before turning and holding up their hands for Kristof to stop.

'Oh fuck, they're on to us,' said Pyotr, looking at Kristof with a panicked face.

'Hold your nerve, Pyotr,' said Kristof, winding down his window for the guard looking up at him.

'Just a minute, we can't have the inner and outer gates open at the same time,' he said, turning his head to watch the inner gate close and lock. 'Ok, move up to the white line and wait for the green light to come on once the outer gates fully open.'

'Ok, thanks,' Kristof said casually. He put the window up and did as instructed, pulling up to the white line. After a couple of minutes that felt like hours, the outer gates slowly started to open, giving a glimpse of the prison carpark and the impending freedom.

'Hey, Oleg, get Valerik out of 103. I'll get these two,' said Demi, selecting the cell key on the bunch chained to his belt and inserting it into the lock. 'Hey, sleepyheads, get yourself up. You're moving prison,' he shouted as he opened the cell door. He stood in the doorway for a few seconds, trying to comprehend why nobody was in the cell.

'Demi, hey, Demi, Valerik's not here. Demi,' came Oleg's panicked voice.

'Sound the alarm, lock the prison down, NOW!' Demi shouted, pulling the radio off his belt.

The outer gate opened its final couple of inches, triggering a green go light in front of them. Kristof released the parking brake and moved the garbage truck slowly forward. He'd only just got off the white line when claxons started sounding. The guards in the courtyard started shouting and the light in front of them went red as the outer gates started to close.

'Fuck, hold on,' shouted Kristof, stamping his foot down on the accelerator, lurching the truck forward.

'Oh, shit, we're not going to make it,' said Pyotr, staring at the ever-narrowing gap between the gates.

'We're going to make it,' growled Kristof through gritted teeth. Tom and John braced themselves against the chairs in front of them.

In the back of the truck, Danny, Valerik and Leonid fell on top of each other as the truck jumped forward. They heard the claxon wailing outside, followed by a loud metallic crash and a horrendous, ear-shattering, metallic scraping noise down each side of the truck as it pulled its way through the closing gates and out into the prison carpark. Kristof moved the truck up a gear and continued to accelerate away from the prison down the approach road.

'Pyotr, call the guys, get them to the garage, we need to ditch this truck and get out of here before the police get roadblocks in place,' shouted Kristof, turning the truck onto the road outside the prison way too hard for the speed they were travelling.

The truck leaned over dangerously. Its rear tyres losing grip, sliding the back end into parked cars, scraping and crushing the door panels, and shattering the windows before the tyres caught and the truck straightened itself.

'For fuck's sake,' yelled Leonid as he somersaulted in the dark and crashed into the opposite side of the truck. A second later Danny and Valerik joined him with grunts and groans in the darkness.

CHAPTER 42

Parked on the road a little way down from the prison, Pasha and Karl waited in their car. Three of their men sat in another vehicle behind them.

'Where are they?' said Karl impatiently.

'The transport van shouldn't be long,' said Pasha, checking his gun as he waited.

'And the two guards know what to do?'

'Yes, they've been paid well. We follow them, pull them over and take the prisoners, then you give them a few blows to the head to make it look good for the police,' said Pasha, chambering a round and sliding the gun into his shoulder holster.

'What's that?' said Karl.

Pasha lowered his window at the sound of the prison alarms. 'What the fuck is going on?' he said, the sound of scraping metal on metal and a revving diesel engine drowning the wailing claxons.

'I don't know. Hang on. Something's coming,' said Karl, spotting the top of the garbage truck moving fast above the wall lining the approach road.

The two of them looked in surprise as the garbage truck hurtled out of the prison approach road, sliding sideways and obliterating a row of parked cars before it straightened up and headed towards them. Looking up as the truck passed by, Pasha's eyes locked with Kristof Turgenev's in the driving seat, both men's faces blank with the unexpected surprise of seeing each other.

'What? Shit, that's fucking Kristof Turgenev,' Pasha said, starting the car.

'I thought you killed him. What's he doing in a garbage truck?'

'Well, he's not collecting the fucking trash, is he, you idiot? He's alive and must have figured a way to get Valerik and Leonid out, maybe even the Englishman,' said Pasha, turning the car around.

'What about the prison transport?'

'Listen to the alarms, brother, the prison's in lockdown, nobody's going in or out,' said Pasha, stopping next to the car that was parked behind them. 'Follow us. Kristof Turgenev is in that garbage truck.'

Flooring the powerful car, Pasha tore off in pursuit of Kristof. The second car turned around quickly and followed close behind them. Pasha took a left where they'd last seen the truck, and caught sight of it again half a mile up the road, a cloud of diesel fumes coming from its exhaust as Kristof red-lined it in every gear. As they closed the gap, Annika Volkov's number displayed on the car's screen, the ring sounding loudly over the speakers.

'Yes,' Pasha answered abruptly.

'The prison governor just called, the Turgenev cousins and Pearson have escaped in a garbage truck,' she yelled, with no attempt to hide her anger.

'I know. Kristof Turgenev is still alive; he's driving the fucking garbage truck. We're chasing them now.'

'What? That cannot be, I saw him burn,' said Annika pausing to think. 'Hurry, Pasha, the police are on their way. This is too big for the commissioner to hide. If they catch them, they will have to arrest them and return them to the prison. I do not want this to happen. You have my permission to kill them, Pasha. I do not care how you do it. Just kill them, and make sure Kristof Turgenev stays dead this time,' said Annika, regaining some composure.

'Yes, boss,' Pasha replied, a smile spreading across his face as Annika hung up. 'Finally we can stop with the fucking games and do our job.'

———————

'Fuck that bastard Pasha. Here he comes. Hold on, I'm going to try to get rid of him,' said Kristof to Pyotr in Russian.

'Hey, what did he say?' said Tom, leaning forward to Pyotr.

'Eh, Annika Volkov's right-hand man, Pasha, he's chasing us, not good.'

With his eye on Pasha's gaining car in the rear-view mirror, Kristof made a right turn, then braked hard to a stop. Crunching the truck into reverse, Kristof hit the gas, picking up speed as he flew backwards towards the junction. A couple of seconds later Pasha came speeding around the corner, his eyes going wide at the sight of the jagged mechanical lifting gear at the rear of the garbage truck bearing down on him. There was a screech and a puff of smoke from locking tyres on tarmac as Pasha jumped on the brakes.

Out of road and out of time, Pasha's car hit the back of the truck, destroying its front end as the car's soft metal panels crumpled on the solid lifting gear. Pasha and Karl momentarily disappeared behind exploding airbags, the surprise and shock temporarily overloading their senses as the truck crunched into first gear and pulled away.

At the very same time, the second car flew round the corner. The driver saw Pasha's car in front of them and panicked, yanking the steering wheel and jamming on the brakes. He sent the car skidding sideways into the back of Pasha's car.

'Open, you bastard, fucking open,' Pasha yelled, kicking the jammed door furiously until it creaked open.

Karl tried to open his door, but it was jammed shut. He gave up after a few kicks and climbed across and out of Pasha's side.

'Back it up, come on, MOVE, he's getting away!' Pasha bellowed at the driver of the other car.

After a couple of attempts, they managed to separate the mangled metal panels so Pasha and Karl could get in and they could head down the road in search of the garbage truck.

'Where the fuck did it go?' said Karl, looking down the side roads as they passed.

'Fuck, fuck, fuck, keep looking. It can't be far away,' yelled Pasha in frustration.

CHAPTER 43

'Are they still following?' Tom asked Kristof.

'No, I think we lost them.'

'I can hear sirens,' said John, winding the window down to listen.

'It's ok, they are still far away. We will be at the garage in a minute,' said Kristof, checking the mirrors again as he spoke.

The tension grew with the sound of the police sirens. By the time they turned into the garage, they sounded only a few streets away. The Mercedes and BMW were parked as before, Kristof's men watching from inside as he drove the garbage truck through the high roller door, rattling it down behind them as soon as it was in. Selecting a lever on the console for the lifting gear, Kristof opened the back section of the garbage truck and hopped out of the cab. The rest of them did the same and rushed to the rear to see Danny, Valerik and Leonid drop to the floor, faces and hands covered in grime and clothes covered in foul smelling trash.

'Alright, Tom, John, come here and give us a hug,' said Danny, grinning through the mess.

'I think we'll pass, mate, you fucking stink.'

The smell didn't stop Kristof embracing his son and nephew with a tear in his eye. They separated after a while and Kristof shouted something in Russian, causing everyone to move.

'Come, we must get out of here, is not safe. We go to the bar, get you cleaned up,' said Pyotr, waving them to the side door.

'Thank you, I owe you one,' said Danny, nodding to Kristof as he went past with Valerik and Leonid.

'Five years ago you killed my worst enemy, and in prison you helped my flesh and blood survive and escape. We are even, my friend, ok?' Kristof said. Danny nodded back and followed him outside.

'Get in that one. Mikhail, you drive. Pyotr, hurry, get in, we go,' Kristof shouted to Danny, Tom and John, and Mikhail, before turning to Pyotr.

They squashed in the back, Tom lowering the window to blow away the stench clinging to Danny's prison clothes.

'What are you trying to say, Tom?' said Danny, grinning as he picked eggshell out of his hair and flung it out the open window.

'I'm not trying, mate, you fucking stink. But it's still good to see you.'

'You too, and Tom, thanks for coming after me. You too, John,' Danny said, giving them a knowing look.

'You've got Howard to thank for that. As soon as we got a lead, he flew straight out here with us. He's the one who found out where you were and put us in contact with Kristof. He'd be here now if it weren't for an emergency back home,' said Tom to Danny's surprise.

'Howard, well fancy that.'

'Which reminds me, there wasn't time to run any of this by him. I'll have to call him as soon as we're safe. We need to get out of here ASAP,' said Tom, silenced by three police cars screaming across in front of them as they waited patiently to turn onto the main road into central Moscow.

'Don't worry, they will block the roads going out of the city, not into the centre. We will be ok at the bar for now,' said Mikhail over his shoulder as he turned to follow Kristof's car.

As they drove on, more police cars wailed past, and the noise of a police helicopter grew louder overhead until it whomped past, heading out towards the prison and the outskirts of the city. Before long they crossed the Moskva River before zigzagging through the side streets and pulling up outside the bar. Kristof, Pyotr and Mikhail were out first, guns held ready, eyes scanning up and down the street for trouble.

'Is good, go inside,' said Mikhail, ducking his head back into the car.

They got out and moved swiftly into the bar, its few customers, mostly old men and the bar staff, not blinking an eyelid as they moved behind the bar and out the back.

'What about them?' Danny said as he was ushered up the stairs.

'Family, do not worry, you are safe here,' said Valerik, looking back at him with a grin.

'Valerik, you and Leonid go clean up. Danny, there is another bathroom upstairs. I will find you some clothes,' said Kristof when they were on the first floor landing. He waited until they had gone and Tom and John were in the sitting room before waving Pyotr and Mikhail over.

'Pyotr, get Mama to prepare some food and drink, then you and Mikhail watch out front, da. Post men either end of the street, they see anything, and I mean anything, I want to know, eh?' Kristof said, his bright blue eyes looking at them intently.

'Yes, boss,' they said in unison.

'Good. And boys?' Kristof said pausing until they looked back up the stairs at him. 'You did good today. I won't forget this.'

The two men smiled back, then continued their way down the stairs.

CHAPTER 44

'What do you mean you lost them?' said Annika, furious at Pasha's failure.

'Old man Kristof drove a garbage truck into us. The car was trashed,' said Pasha, calmly glancing down at the marble worktop where he'd killed Ustin, before deliberately turning slowly to look behind him.

'What are you doing?' said Annika, pacing around the kitchen island.

'I'm just checking nobody's standing behind me with a gun to my head,' said Pasha dryly, his face deadly serious.

'Don't be so dramatic, Pasha, just find them and kill them,' said Annika, drumming her fingernails on the worktop.

'I need more men. I need to move through Moscow, no stone unturned. Kristof has been hiding somewhere in the city all the time we thought he was dead. Someone has to know where he is.'

'You will have your men. Now go, pay them, torture them, or kill them. I don't care. Do whatever it takes to loosen their tongues,' Annika said, spinning on her heels and walking briskly out of the room, her clicking footsteps growing faint on the hard marble.

Pasha waited until she could no longer be heard. He breathed in a big sigh, straightened his suit jacket and headed out of the mansion. His family had served the Volkovs for generations, his father with Sebastian Volkov as he ruled with a fist of iron, and him with Viktor and Yuri as they fought and failed to take London. It was their underestimation that eventually cost them their lives. Now he served Annika. Half the time he wanted to snap her pretty little neck, the other half he wanted to help her grow and succeed, his wealth and status across Moscow growing with her.

He walked out the front where five cars sat on the vast drive. Twenty men milled around them, armed with handguns and Kalashnikov AK47's. The relaxed chat changed in an instant at the approach of Pasha, and a tense professionalism took its place. Hard men who were no strangers to death and violence looked back at him.

'Load up, we will start in the Khamovniki District. Kristof used to have a strip club and bars there,' shouted Pasha, walking up to the passenger side of the nearest car and getting in the front. 'Go,' he said to Karl, slamming the door.

The others didn't need telling twice. They moved swiftly to the cars, got in and fell into line behind Pasha's vehicle as it drove through the mansion gates, turned onto the road and headed for central Moscow.

CHAPTER 45

om and John sat waiting for Danny to get cleaned up. Tom's phone rang. The number was withheld, but he had a pretty good idea who it was.

'Afternoon, boss,' he said.

'It's still morning this end, Tomas. How did your meeting with Kristof Turgenev go? Did you get word to Daniel?' Howard said, with an unaccustomed weariness in his voice.

'Er, yeah, about that, he's er—'

'Oh Christ, don't tell me he's dead,' said Howard, deflated.

'No, no, er, we, er, broke him out of jail this morning in a garbage truck, he's here with us at Kristof's place,' said Tom preparing himself for the twenty questions about to come.

'You did what! You didn't think to run this by me? Did you stop for one minute and think about the implications if you'd been caught? Christ, man, you could have caused a diplomatic nightmare. Remember the Novichok incident in Amesbury.'

'Sorry, boss, there wasn't time. We had a short window of opportunity and I made a judgement call,' said Tom, only half-heartedly apologising.

'Mmm, well at least you didn't get caught. What about Daniel, is he ok?' Howard said, calming down again.

'He's fine, he's upstairs washing garbage out of his hair.'

'Right, you'll need an evacuation plan. Sit tight, I'll get back to you as soon as I can.'

'Yes, boss, thanks,' said Tom lowering the phone and looking at John. 'That went better than expected.'

'Yeah, wait until we get back. The boss'll have us on shit duties for the foreseeable for not telling him,' said John with a grin.

'Doesn't matter. Danny's saved both our lives in the past and there's no way he would have left us in that prison to rot,' said Tom, frowning

'Agreed, but it doesn't stop us copping the crap when we get back home.'

'Who's copping the crap?' said Danny, walking into the room looking decidedly fresher than he did earlier.

'Ah, it's nothing, we've just told the boss the good news,' said Tom.

'I'm guessing he was his usual bundle of fun,' said Danny with a smirk.

'Yeah, he's working on an evac to get us home.'

'Good, you should get out of Moscow as soon as possible,' came Kristof's voice from behind them.

'What about you?' said Danny, locking eyes with him.

'Moscow is our home. The Turgenevs have been fighting for control of it for decades. If it's not the Volkovs it would be someone else, it's the way it is here,' he said with a shrug.

The room went into reflective silence, before Kristof

broke into a wide grin. 'But that battle is for tomorrow. Today I have my family back. We celebrate,' Kristof said, walking out the door and shouting down the stairs in Russian.

Moments after he returned Pyotr entered carrying a big tray of food while a little old lady carrying a bottle of Stoli vodka and glasses jabbered on at him. As they placed them onto the table Valerik and Leonid entered the room. The old lady's face lit up when she saw them. There was an exchange of fast-spoken Russian before they kissed her on the cheek and she shuffled out of the room.

'My grandmother thanks you for helping to bring us home,' said Valerik filling up a glass of vodka before downing it in one. 'Ah, that tastes good. Here, drink, eat.'

As they ate, drank and relaxed, Danny couldn't help noticing Kristof wasn't drinking. He sat near the window, glancing up and down the road periodically, trying not to make it obvious he was doing so.

'Expecting visitors?' said Danny, sitting beside him.

'Always,' he replied with a half-smile.

'What are you going to do about Annika Volkov?' said Danny bluntly.

'I'd like to put a bullet in the bitch's forehead, but it's not that easy, she's well protected. She's rebuilt the Volkov mansion like a fortress and is always guarded when she is out. But I fear the question at the moment is what are you going to do about Annika Volkov? You know she will come after you. You killed her family, her blood. Family honour demands it. No, my friend, she wants you dead far more than she wants me.'

'I know, but back home it'll be on my own ground and my rules. She won't get the jump on me again,' said Danny, tensing as he thought about it.

'Then put a bullet in her head for me,' said Kristof,

raising a glass to Danny. 'Nostrovia.'

'Nostrovia,' said Danny, his face softening as he returned the gesture.

Over the other side of the room, Tom's phone rang, the number withheld as usual.

'Boss,' Tom answered.

'Tomas, I need you, John and Daniel to get to Novinka Airfield for midday tomorrow. It's around a hundred miles due south of Moscow. I've arranged for a light aircraft to fly you to a small airfield just outside Kiev. You can make your way to Kiev International Airport and fly home from there,' said Howard.

'Thanks, boss, I'll call you from Kiev,' Tom said.

'Yes, please do. Oh, and Tomas?'

'Yes, boss?'

'Good job,' said Howard, to Tom's surprise.

'Thanks, boss,' said Tom hanging up.

'What's the plan?' said Danny, watching him from across the room.

'The boss has got us a ride into the Ukraine from an airfield way south of here, a place called Novinka. Pickup's tomorrow midday. We can get a flight from Kiev International home.'

'What about my passport?' Danny said, frowning.

'It's at our hotel with mine and John's, we'll go and get them and check out. Are we ok to stay here tonight, Kristof?'

'Da, my house is your house. Pyotr will take you to the hotel,' said Kristof, nodding to Pyotr.

'Leonid and I will drive you to Novinka in the morning,' said Valerik, chipping in beside them.

'Thank you,' said Danny.

'Come, I take you to hotel,' said Pyotr getting up and moving to the door.

CHAPTER 46

Logged into the secure portal on his laptop, James Bullman listened to the one-sided conversation between Howard and Tom. He scribbled the words 'Novinka Airfield noon tomorrow' on a notepad and reached for his jacket pocket, pulling away when he remembered he'd ditched his burner phone because of Howard's relentless probing into his business affairs. Sitting back in his office chair, a thought crossed his mind, throwing the frown on his face into a devious smile.

If Howard's golden boy dies and two UK Secret Service agents are found on Russian soil undertaking an unsanctioned mission, Russia will demand answers from the UK government, and Howard will be thrown out on his arse faster than his feet can carry him. Two birds taken care of with one stone.

Closing the laptop down, he tore the page off the notepad, folded it, and put it in his pocket before leaving his office. He smiled at a colleague as they passed in the corridor, then paused and called back, 'I say, Henry, is Barrington back from holiday yet?'

'Er, I don't think so, not until Monday,' Henry shouted back, still moving down the corridor.

'Ok, thank you, Henry,' said James, waiting until he'd disappeared out of sight before he turned back the way he'd come.

Passing his own office, James continued down the corridor, glancing both ways before entering Kenneth Barrington's empty office. He shut the door behind him and moved to the desk, fishing his little black address book out of his jacket pocket. James dialled a number on Barrington's office phone. It clicked with an international dialling tone before ringing.

'Come on, you ice cold bitch, answer your—' said James, infuriated at the length of time it took Annika to answer her phone.

'Yes, who is this?' she said in Russian.

'Er, hello, Annika, it's James Bullman,' said James, automatically falling into diplomatic politeness.

'Mr Bullman, how unexpected. I didn't think I would hear from you again. What do you want?' Annika said, in her monotone and unemotional English.

'I heard about your little fiasco at Lefortovo Prison and wanted to offer my support.'

'If you're calling to gloat, Mr Bullman, I must warn you against it,' she spat back before he had time to finish.

'No, no. My dear Annika, I'm calling to help you,' said James, still being cagey as he enjoyed the upper hand his information gave him.

'Help me how?' she replied, growing slightly annoyed by James's games.

'I know where Daniel Pearson will be at noon tomorrow,' he said, pausing for her anticipated surprise and adulation.

'And what is it you want for this information?' Annika

replied without the slightest hint of either, leaving James to nurture his bruised ego.

'Mr Pearson has two English Secret Service agents travelling with him. Do what you will with Pearson, but I want the two agents found by the authorities with a set of papers I'm about to send you.'

'Tell me where he will be,' said Annika coldly.

'Do we have a deal,' said James, pushing the point.

'Yes, we have a deal. Now tell me where they will be tomorrow at noon.'

'They will be at an airfield in Novinka, about a hundred miles south of Moscow. A small aircraft will be coming to fly them across the border to the Ukraine,' said James, feeling a little smug.

'You know this for sure?'

'A one hundred percent certainty, my dear.'

'Ok, send me the papers,' Annika said, hanging up without waiting for a reply.

Bloody ungrateful Russian bitch.

Taking a handkerchief out of his lapel pocket, James wiped the phone and receiver down and slid out of Kenneth Barrington's office. Thankfully the corridor was empty as James moved back to his own office. He opened his laptop and logged into his secure portal.

Hmm, a few low-level official documents and an order from Howard to collect intelligence on...on...on...let me think, ah yes, the high-level storage facility north of the city, that will do nicely.

He smiled to himself as he compiled the papers before sending them to Annika Volkov. Pleased with himself, he logged out and turned his laptop off. Looking out of the window at the sun streaming through the clouds over the London skyline, James decided to celebrate his own ingeniousness with a visit to a very discreet club he occasionally frequented. It was a club for clients with very specific inter-ests, the kind of interests that had got James into trouble with the Volkovs in the first place, but try as he might to refrain from his lust and perversions, eventually they got the better of him and dragged him back in.

CHAPTER 47

The Khamovniki bakery van pulled up to the rear loading doors and stopped. Karl got out of the driver's seat and moved to the loading door, giving it a couple of good bangs. A few seconds later Igor rattled the chain as he pulled it, raising the up and over door. From the passenger side of the van, two more of Annika Volkov's men got out and joined Karl.

'Did you get them all?' said Igor, matter-of-fact.

'Yeah, apart from Ruben, he spotted us as we turned up and ran out the back,' said Karl, pulling the back doors open.

Four men lay hogtied and shaking on the floor of the van, cloth sacks pulled over their heads. Clicking a flick knife open, Karl dragged the nearest body towards him and cut his feet free.

'Get up, move,' Karl growled, pushing him to one of his men to take him inside.

'Please, I don't know anything, please,' came the muffled plea from the next man as Karl dragged him closer to the back doors and cut his legs free.

Karl powered his fist into the cloth sack over the man's head before he could start whining again. 'Shut up, you don't speak until we tell you to,' yelled Karl, grabbing the stunned man under the armpit and hoisting him upright before pushing him towards Igor.

He repeated the process with the other two men before guiding all four of them roughly through the loading bay and into the working area of the bakery. They pushed the men back against the wall, removed their hoods and backed away, leaving them petrified and blinking at the sudden intrusion of light. As the bakery came into focus, the men started to physically shake at the sight of Pasha standing in front of them. He had his suit jacket off and one of the bakery aprons on over his crisp white shirt. His sleeves were rolled up and his twin Glock 17s were visible under each arm in their black leather shoulder holsters. Stains and splashes of arterial blood crisscrossed his front, overspilling the apron to show bright red on his shirt. Three bloody, mutilated bodies lay at his feet, their faces contorted in their final moments of agony.

'Gentlemen, welcome. I'm going to ask you a question and I hope for your sake you give me a better answer than your predecessors,' Pasha said, his voice calm but his eyes full of crazed menace.

'What do you want with us? We've always paid Miss Volkov on time,' one of them said, his voice weak and his eyes pleading.

Karl was in like a shot, his sideways blow to the man's temple flooring him instantly.

'I told you, you do not fucking speak until we tell you to,' Karl yelled, kicking the downed man for good measure.

'Bring him here, Karl.'

Picking him up off the floor like a rag doll, Karl stood him up, wheezing in front of Pasha.

'Where is Kristof Turgenev?' Pasha said, leaning in so his nose almost touched the man's.

'Turgenev, I, I don't know, I swear I don't. I thought he was dead,' the man stammered.

Pasha backed away. He moved to a machine on his left and punched the on button. When the man turned his head his eyes went wide at the sight of the industrial bread slicer, its blades vibrating noisily in the centre of the stainless steel top where the bread moved through.

'Where's Turgenev?' Pasha growled while Karl pushed the man towards the machine as he struggled futilely with his hands tied behind his back.

'No, I don't know, I swear, please,' the man screamed, a dark patch appearing at his crotch as he pissed himself.

Pasha put his hand on the back of the man to match Karl's. They slapped him onto the stainless steel top inches away from the blades.

'Last chance, where's Turgenev?'

'I swear on my children's lives, I don't know. Please, I'd tell you if I did,' screamed the man in desperation, tears rolling down his cheeks.

Pasha gave a nod to Karl and the two of them thrust the man's head forward. He screamed for a while as the machine struggled to cut though hair and bone and brain before it jammed with his head half-in and half-sliced, blood dripping out the other side. Leaving him, Pasha turned to the others.

'Where's Kristof Turgenev?' he repeated coldly.

'I don't know, but we heard a rumour he was still alive, somewhere in the Zamoskvorechye district, a bar or something,' said one of the other men, his words spilling out at lightning speed as he looked horrified at the mess stuck in the bread slicer.

'Good, good, see this is progress. Would anyone else

like to add to that?' Pasha said, pausing at the sound of his mobile ringing in the pocket of his jacket hung over the back of a chair. 'Excuse me one minute,' he added, getting the phone out to answer it. 'Yes.'

'Get everyone back here, Pasha. I know where Pearson will be tomorrow,' came Annika's emotionless voice.

'I'm going to Zamoskvorechye. I have a lead on Kristof,' said Pasha gruffly.

'No, you won't. You will come back here. Do you hear me, Pasha. I don't want Pearson warned off by you and your men crashing around Zamoskvorechye district like a herd of elephants. Once we deal with Pearson, you can hunt that rat Kristof down,' said Annika with an angry outburst that she quickly got under control.

Pasha stood motionless with the phone to his ear. He glared angrily at the three terrified men opposite him. Without warning he drew his Glock 17 in a flash and emptied the clip into the three of them.

'On our way,' he said, watching them slide to the floor. Ending the call he holstered his gun and took the apron off, throwing it to the floor.

'Torch the place, we are done here,' he said storming out of the bakery.

CHAPTER 48

think the bloody Russians have poisoned me again,' said John, rubbing his head.

'You and me both,' said Danny, looking up from his coffee.

'How much vodka did we drink last night?' said Tom, following John into the dining room at Kristof's place.

'Too much,' said Danny as the other two sat down, nurturing their own strong coffees.

'Fuck, my mouth feels like the bottom of a budgie cage,' said Tom, taking a big swig.

All heads turned at the sound of footsteps moving swiftly up the stairs from the bar below.

'Hey, sleepyheads, you look like shit, da,' laughed Valerik, fresh as a daisy.

'Yeah, yeah, laugh it up. When do we leave?' said Danny, managing a smile.

'Soon. Leonid and my father are getting the cars ready, he's decided to come with us,' said Valerik, something in his voice ringing alarm bells with Danny.

'What's up?'

Valerik paused, his face growing deadly serious. 'A bakery not far from here was torched yesterday. They found eight bodies inside, tied, tortured and shot. Rumour has it, it was Volkov's men looking for us. It's not safe here anymore. We will take you to the airport and move base. Drink your coffee. We leave soon.' Valerik turned and left the room, avoiding further conversation on the subject, leaving Danny and the others looking at each other uneasily across the table.

'It doesn't seem right leaving them to deal with Annika Volkov's men,' Danny eventually said, looking at them intensely.

'Don't give me that look, Danny. We're in a foreign country, you're wanted, we have no backup and no plan. We're going home, and if Annika Volkov comes after you, we'll be ready. Ok?' said Tom, pushing the point.

The room went silent once more. Danny held Tom's gaze for a few seconds before draining the rest of his coffee and banging down the empty mug.

'Ok. Let's go home,' he eventually said, getting up.

Tom and John followed him downstairs into the bar. Kristof was there, his jacket barely covering his holstered Makarov pistols. Although he smiled as they approached, Danny could tell he was on edge.

'Pyotr,' he shouted over his shoulder.

Seconds later Pyotr appeared beside him with a canvas bag in his hand. He opened it, pulled out a handgun by the barrel and passed it to Danny. 'Just a precaution,' he said, pulling another gun out for Tom and then for John.

'Right, we've got to go. It is a long journey. Danny, you go with Valerik and Leonid in front. You two come with me and Pyotr,' said Kristof, leading them outside to the two waiting Mercedes 4x4s.

Danny nodded to Tom and John as he left them to get

into the front car with Valerik and Leonid. The minute he was in, Leonid started pulling the car away with Kristof following close behind. The two of Kristof's men they passed at the end of the street didn't go unnoticed by Danny as they turned onto the main road and headed out of the city.

'How bad is it?' said Danny, leaning forward to talk to Valerik as he drove.

'No offence, my friend, I owe you a debt of gratitude and like having you around, but I think it will be a lot safer here once you are on that plane out of Russia,' said Valerik grinning at Danny in the rear-view mirror.

'None taken,' said Danny, watching row upon row of grey apartment blocks as they headed out of Moscow.

Suburbia gave way to miles of thick forest, broken up with the odd town as they drove along the motorway heading south. Valerik kept in the slower lanes, driving carefully, never going over the speed limit. A little way back, Kristof followed, mirroring them as they moved to overtake slow lorries and cars.

'How far is Novinka Airfield from here?' said Danny after an hour or so.

'Er, is about forty minutes away, don't worry, we will be there in plenty of time for the plane,' said Leonid, turning to look back at Danny.

'Why don't you come with us? I've got contacts. I could get you passports and papers. Start a new life in the UK.'

Leonid just grinned back at him, 'No, my friend, believe me, if we wanted to leave we could get our own papers. Moscow is our home. It was my father's home and his father's home before him. It will take more than some poor imitation of her father to run us out. Our day will come, we will run Moscow once more.'

'Damn right, cousin,' said Valerik, banging his hands on the steering wheel.

'Ok, fair enough,' said Danny, sitting back in his seat.

They travelled in silence for quite some time, each man lost in their own thoughts. Eventually the sign appeared for Novinka Airfield. They turned off the motorway and headed through the forest. Danny knew they were getting close when his eyes followed a small single-engine plane as it passed over the top of the car, disappearing in the distance as it descended below the treeline to land.

CHAPTER 49

A s the road swept around a wide bend, a collection of small aircraft hangers came into view, shortly followed by light aircraft, the runway, and some more small buildings on the far side. Being a small private airfield there was no security gate as they turned through the entrance and drove between the row of hangars. Danny could see the plane that had just landed, it was standing by a hangar on the far end, its propellers still spinning but no pilot in sight.

The hairs on the back of Danny's neck stood up as alarm bells rang in his head. He swung his head and spotted two aircraft mechanics with their backs to him inside the hangar to his right, the collars of their blue overalls up and the peaks of their baseball caps pulled down low over their faces. Darting his head to the left, Danny caught sight of two more men in overalls and caps. They were in mid-turn with ShAK12 urban assault rifles in their arms.

Shit, it's a kill box.

'Hit the gas. Go, go! It's a fucking trap!' Danny yelled,

whipping the gun Pyotr had given him up before his words sunk in with Valerik and Leonid.

He fired off three rounds in quick succession through the closed car window at the men as they raised their rifles, the deafening noise in the confined space causing Valerik to snake all over the tarmac before he floored the accelerator.

Danny was already spinning away to the right as one of the guys in the hangar flew backwards with two bullets in the centre of his chest. The other man spun around clutching his neck as one of Danny's bullets tore through its side, a fountain of arterial blood splaying out between his fingers.

Focused on the right-hand hangar, Danny's eyes found the two men just as they aimed their rifles at him. He threw himself flat on the back seat as streams of automatic fire ripped around him. Metallic popping noises filled the air as bullets punched through the thin sheet metal body panels. He could feel the heat and displacement of air as bullets passed millimetres from his face before punching holes out through the other side of the car. In the front passenger seat, Leonid's body jerked and convulsed as the bullets found their target, killing him instantly. A bullet blew the front tyre out, sliding the vehicle sideways towards the end hangar and the airplane with its propellers still spinning. Fighting with the steering wheel, Valerik managed to swerve the plane but couldn't stop the car in time to avoid hitting the hangar door with the rear side. The impact wrenched their bodies to one side as the car spun inside the hangar, out of control, stopping abruptly as it hit the front wheel of a stored aircraft.

———

A little way back, Kristof watched the men in the hangar rip holes in his son's car.

'Aaaargh. Die, you fuckers!' he yelled at the top of his voice.

Leaning forward, he gripped the steering wheel so tight his knuckle went white and pulled it hard to the right, squealing the tyres as he stamped on the gas.

'Whoa, whoa, Kristof, what are you doing?' shouted Tom from the back.

Aiming straight at the gunmen in the hangar, Kristof blanked Tom and held fast. By the time the two men's attention broke away from Valerik's car, Kristof was upon them. He hit one man head-on, destroying his legs before throwing him over the bonnet with such force his head shattered the windscreen with a sickening thud before he disappeared over the roof. His fellow gunman tried desperately to dive to safety. He managed to get his body clear before the front of the car hit his legs, shattering them as he spun off violently. Kristof jammed on the brakes, locking the wheels up on the painted concrete floor. He skidded into rows of red Snap On tool chests before ploughing into the rear wall, setting off the multitude of air bags in the car.

———

Kicking the door open, Danny was out of the vehicle in a flash. He had his gun held steady across the car roof, covering the open hangar door. When nothing moved he went to the driver's door and tried to open it. When it didn't open he put the gun on the car roof and grabbed the handle with both hands, pulling it with all his might. It opened with a metal-on-metal creak to reveal Valerik's stunned and blood-covered face blinking at him.

'Are you hurt, Valerik? Are you hurt?' Danny said, trying to see if the blood was from Leonid's limp body beside him or whether Valerik had been hit himself.

'Er, no. No, I'm ok. Leonid,' he said, turning to look at his cousin.

'He's gone. You can grieve him later. If we're going to get out of here alive, I need you to stick close to me,' Danny said, getting his attention back.

'Yes, ok,' said Valerik, moving to get out.

'Good. Pass me Leonid's gun and any spare magazines. Quickly, there'll be more coming for us,' Danny said, his mind assessing the situation as he searched the gaps between the light aircraft around them for signs of more gunmen.

'Here,' Valerik said, handing Danny Leonid's gun and two magazines.

'Thanks. Try calling your father and the others, find out where they are, I'm going to take a look outside the hangar,' said Danny. He slid the magazines into his back pockets before heading towards the doors, weaving between the light aircraft for cover, both guns locked rigid in his arms in front of him.

CHAPTER 50

Further down the airfield, past a row of smaller single-plane hangars, Annika looked out the window of the control room perched on top of a square brick building.

'What's happening, Pasha?' she demanded impatiently.

Pasha ignored her as he tried to listen to his earpiece. 'Ivan, you take half the men and close in on hangar four. Karl, you take the other half and move on hangar two,' he ordered.

'Pasha,' Annika barked, her temper boiling over.

'What?' Pasha yelled, his tolerance of his ever-demanding boss wearing thin. His yell and murderous look silenced her, leaving them in a standoff as they glared at each other.

'I would just like to know what is going on,' she finally said, her voice cold and controlled once more.

'We will have them soon. They are divided and trapped inside two separate hangars,' Pasha said, his attention turning back to the viewing window and his earpiece.

Annika stood a few paces behind him, wondering if

Pasha's growing belligerence meant he'd outlived his usefulness to her.

———

In hangar number two, Tom was out of the car first, closely followed by John. Keeping low, he moved through the tool chests and stored planes, his eyes searching until he found the ShAK12 urban assault rifle from the man they'd ploughed down.

'John, find the other one,' he said, looking back and pointing to the other side of the hangar and the screams of pain coming from the gunman with the shattered legs.

'Roger that,' said John, heading off. Pyotr limped after him, his knee swelling up after breaking the glove box with it in the crash.

Behind them, Kristof looked at his ringing phone.

'Valerik, is that you, are you ok?' he said, struggling to get the words out quick enough.

'Yes, Papa, I'm ok, but Leonid, he's dead, Papa, he's dead,' said Valerik, emotional at the loss of his cousin.

'Those fucking bastards. What about Danny? Is he still alive?'

'Yes, he's gone to check outside.'

'Ok, sit tight. We'll come to you,' said Kristof, pulling his gun and moving towards the others.

Over the top of the injured man's screams and the airplane with its engine running outside Danny's hangar, Tom heard vehicle noises and doors slamming. He slid behind a long metal tool bench and poked his head out to see through the hangar doors. Eight men with assault rifles had lined themselves up behind two Audi SUVs on the far side of the tarmac by the other hangars. Tom tucked himself back behind the heavy metal tool bench just as they opened fire in a deafening hail of white-hot metal. Tom curled up as tight as he could with his arm over his face as bullets whizzed over the work bench and ricocheted around him.

'John,' Tom yelled at the top of his voice when the volley of fire ceased.

'I'm ok, Pyotr's gone,' John yelled back from his position, tucked behind one of the large upright girders by the door that made up the hangar's structure.

'Kristof, you ok?' yelled Tom.

'Yeah, a bullet grazed my shoulder but I'm ok.'

'John, on three you go left to right; I'll go right to left. Single shots, pick your targets well, ok?' shouted Tom, popping up into a squat behind the workbench.

'Roger that,' came John's yelled reply.

'One. Two. Three.'

Both men moved up. Tom moved his rifle over the bench using the metal surface to steady his aim while John swung around the girder and leaned on it to steady himself. Being trained and seasoned combat soldiers, Tom and John's eyes locked on their targets as they breathed steady and squeezed their triggers simultaneously, striking the men at each end with a headshot. They'd already moved to the next target before the men hit the ground and the plume of red mist had cleared the air. They hit the next two men just as the remaining four comprehended what had happened and opened fire, sending Tom and John behind cover again.

———

Reaching the door, Danny saw the four men Tom and John downed. As those remaining let rip in return, Danny tucked a gun into the back of his jeans then aimed the other with both hands locked together and arms outstretched. He slowed his breathing and blanked out the noise of the airplane engine to his left. Exhaling and holding his breath, Danny squeezed off shot after shot at Volkov's men. At that range with a handgun, accuracy was difficult to obtain, but halfway through the magazine, Danny moved target a fraction as one man dropped with a fountain of blood pumping from an artery on the side of his neck. On the last bullet, just before the gun clicked empty, Danny caught the next man in the forearm as he leaned across the bonnet of the SUV with his rifle.

That'll even the odds up.

Expelling the empty magazine, Danny pulled a spare out of his jeans pocket. As he turned his head, he caught the reflection in the plane's cockpit window of two of Volkov's men coming around the corner of the hangar behind him. Turning and sliding the magazine home in one movement, Danny put two in the chest of the man in front. As the man fell back, his accomplice pushed him forward with all his might, hurtling the body into Danny, knocking him down.

Danny's arm swung wide as he fell, the gun ripping from his fingers as its barrel ventured into the path of the spinning propeller blades. The man standing over him levelled his gun, a smile creeping across his face. Time went into slow motion. Helpless, Danny could see the muscles in the man's gun hand tense as he started to pull the trigger. At that same moment, Valerik exploded out of the hanger, shoving the gunman with all his might into the airplane's spinning propeller blades. Shock and horror locked on the his face forever as the blades tore him into shredded pieces from his groin to his neck, leaving a sprayed bloody line heading out from either side of the plane, as the centrifugal force threw the blood off the spinning propellers.

'Thanks,' Danny said, springing to his feet and tucking back behind the hangar door.

Valerik nodded in acknowledgement then cocked his head towards the corner of the hangar. 'Over here,' he said, moving to a big tarpaulin-covered object. Pulling it off, he uncovered a big red pickup truck. When he opened the door, the pilot from the plane outside flopped out with a bullet hole in his forehead.

'Keys,' Danny said.

Valerik took a peek into the pickup and shook his head.

'Let's check his pockets,' Danny said, bending down to go through the jacket while Valerik went through the trouser pockets.

'Hey, jackpot,' said Valerik, jangling a bunch of keys.

CHAPTER 51

Pasha smashed his fists down on the radar monitor in the control room. Filled with rage, he whipped out his gun and shot the tied-up air traffic controller in the head before composing himself and putting the gun away again.

'What do you mean they've shot six of our men? Fuck it, Karl, hit them with the truck,' said Pasha, giving a sideways glance at Annika, daring her to challenge him.

'Ok, I'm on my way,' said Karl over a revving diesel engine.

'Ivan, where the hell are you?' continued Pasha.

'I've just forced the fire exit door at the rear of the hangar. I'm going to get them from behind while the rest of the men keep them busy at the hangar doors.'

'Good, good, kill the bastards,' said Pasha with growing confidence.

———

'Get down!' yelled Danny.

Valerik reacted instantly. Dropping down beside the pickup, Danny's gun was level and steady by the time he was halfway to the floor. He'd squeezed off four rounds at Volkov's men as they ventured into the hangar, hitting and killing one while catching the second in the shoulder as he dived back out.

'Call your father and tell him we're coming for...' said Danny, his words tailing off. He'd heard something or sensed something, a noise, a movement behind him at the back of the hangar. 'Start the truck, I'll be back in a minute.'

Danny peeled off and disappeared behind the planes and tool benches before Valerik could question him. Doing as Danny asked, Valerik got in the pickup truck and started it. Pointing his gun out the car window with one hand and his phone in the other, he made the call.

———

Kristof emptied his magazine at the SUVs before answering his phone.

'Valerik.'

'Sit tight, Papa, we've got a vehicle, we're coming to get you,' said Valerik, letting off a couple of shots as another of Volkov's men swung his gun around the opening, shooting wildly before tucking back out of sight.

'Ok,' said Kristof, watching a small tanker move into view near the SUVs. It moved slowly, turning to point straight at them, a trail of aviation fuel spilling from an open valve behind it. The driver's door opened and Karl jumped from the cab and rolled away. As the tanker rumbled towards them, Karl fired his gun at the trail of high-octane fuel, sending a river of chasing flame towards the source.

'Valerik, kill them, kill them all!' Kristof shouted, dropping the phone.

He and Tom reacted instantly, turning and running towards the rear of the hangar in a desperate effort to avoid the approaching tanker. Pinned down by gunfire, all John could do was watch helplessly as the tanker rolled inside, crashing into the small planes as the chasing flame caught up with its source. The explosion was earth-shattering, destroying the hangar and everything in it, in one all-encompassing fireball.

———

Danny steadied himself as everything around him shook. Still focused, he caught a brief glimpse of Ivan between the aircraft. He was creeping his way towards Valerik as he shouted down the phone for his father. Somewhere overhead he heard the noise of an aircraft. It sounded like it was coming into land, changing its mind last minute as it throttled back to take it up and away again. Probably scared off after seeing the explosion. He looked at his G-Shock watch, 12:00 p.m.

Shit, there goes my ride.

Turning his attention back to Ivan, Danny moved around a row of tall metal lockers. As he moved out the other end, he came face to face with him, shock, surprise and reaction all happening in a split second. Both men whipped their guns up and grabbed the wrist of the other's gun hand, locked in stalemate by each other's vice-like grip. Shots fired off, punching holes in the metal lockers and a plane's cockpit. Danny went in for a headbutt, but Ivan dodged it and countered with a knee to Danny's ribs, knocking the wind out of him. Fighting the reflex to double over, Danny smashed Ivan's gun hand down onto the corner of a metal workbench, causing him to release the gun, which rattled off out of sight.

Trained in the formidable Spetsnaz, Russian Special Forces, Ivan ripped his hand free from Danny's grip and powered his fist into the side of Danny's neck. The pain was intense. He saw stars in front of his eyes and was only vaguely aware of the second and third blows to his head. The gun fell from his hand and his legs buckled. Sucking up as much air as possible, Danny landed on his knee and threw an upper cut to Ivan's balls with all his might. The blow caused the big man to stagger back, knocking a tray of tools across the workbench as he doubled-up, groaning.

The vital seconds gave Danny time to shake away some of the dizziness and go on the attack. He powered forward, ducking under Ivan's attempts to block him as he unleashed a blistering combination of punches to Ivan's torso. Just when he thought he had the advantage, Ivan grabbed Danny in an explosion of movement and hurled him flat on his back onto the steel workbench. Before Danny could react, Ivan had his hands around his throat, crushing his windpipe with a grip of steel. Danny punched at Ivan's body and pulled at his arms, trying to free himself. He started to feel lightheaded and stars started to dance across his eyes for the second time in only a few minutes. Slapping his hands down onto the workbench, he frantically scrabbled around until he felt a rubber handle. Grabbing it, Danny punched it upwards into Ivan's neck. He felt it cut through the resistance of skin, muscle and bone until only the rubber handle was sticking out of Ivan's neck.

Ivan made a raspy, gurgling sound as he released his grip on Danny. He staggered back a step or two and grabbed the rubber handle, pulling the object slowly out of his neck. Danny watched as the blood-covered screwdriver emerged, a fountain of arterial blood erupting from the hole it had been plugging. Staring at Danny in disbelief, the colour drained from Ivan's face as his eyes rolled back in his head and he dropped to the ground. After catching a few deep breaths, Danny searched Ivan, taking his phone and the radio and earpiece, before picking up his gun and heading to the front of the hangar and Valerik in the pickup truck. Sliding into the passenger seat, he could see something was wrong by the tears in Valerik's eyes and the phone trembling in his fingers.

'They're all dead. They killed them all,' he said sullenly.

Danny sat for a second, then slid the earpiece on and held the radio to his mouth.

"I'm coming for you."

CHAPTER 52

van, Ivan, what's happening, where the fuck are you?'
Pasha growled down the mic.

The tension became unbearable as Pasha listened
to the crashing and grunts of Danny and Ivan's fight. It
ended in a deathly, raspy, gurgling sound, then silence.

'I'm coming for you,' came Danny's voice, calm, low
and with controlled menace.

Pasha didn't move for a few seconds. A feeling of fear
crept over him. It was alien to him. He hadn't felt it since
childhood, since his father had beaten him black and blue.
The sight of the red pickup truck hammering out of the
hangar shook him into action.

'We must go, NOW,' he said angrily to Annika.

She opened her mouth to protest, but the shock of
Pasha grabbing her wrist and dragging her out of the
control room silenced her.

'Karl, we're leaving,' he ordered over the radio.

'On my way,' came Karl's response.

'Pasha, how dare you treat me like this? He's not dead.
I want you to kill him,' Annika said, finding her voice as

Pasha released her wrist to open the car door. He slammed it the second she was in and hurried around to the driver's side.

'This man is bad luck. He killed your family and he will kill us all if we don't get out of here,' Pasha said, watching the speeding pickup as it skidded sideways on the tarmac, before coming straight towards them.

Starting up the powerful Mercedes, Pasha threw it into drive and slammed his foot to the floor.

———

'Keep your foot down,' said Danny to Valerik.

'I'm going to rip that bitch's head off,' Valerik said through gritted teeth.

Danny wound the window down and leaned out the passenger side. He tried to steady himself against the erratic movement of the pickup as he eyed Pasha's car tyres down the sights of his gun. He squeezed off round after round until the magazine was empty. They went wide of the target, missing the wheel to punch neat round holes in the surrounding body panels. Ducking back inside the pickup, Danny had ejected the empty magazine and pulled the last full one from his jeans pocket before his arse hit the seat. Slamming in the new magazine on his way back out the window, Danny had the Mercedes in his sights in seconds. Locking his arm at the target, Danny remained calm and squeezed the trigger, hitting the tyre with the fourth shot. The Mercedes snaked wildly out of control before sliding off the road and spinning on the grass into the perimeter fence. Ducking inside the pickup, Danny and Valerik looked ahead, stony-faced, as they closed in on Annika and Pasha.

To their surprise, the two bullet-ridden SUVs that had

kept them pinned down earlier hurtled out from between two small hangars. Karl cornered hard, heading for Pasha and Annika, his tyres squealing as they fought for grip. The SUV with Volkov's two remaining men accelerated straight at Danny and Valerik, striking the pickup truck in the rear quarter. The impact sent the vehicle spinning into the roller door of the hangar beside them, bending it inwards until it ripped off the runners on either side with a horrific screeching of metal against metal. The second they stopped, Valerik was out of the driver's seat and firing his gun at the approaching SUV. With his door jammed by pieces of metal, Danny slid out of the shattered passenger window and clambered over to join him.

Hole after hole punched through the windscreen of the vehicle until Valerik's gun clicked empty, the bullets continuing their journey through the soft flesh of the driver and passenger, killing them instantly. In the sudden quietness, the SUV rolled to one side of them, stopping dead as it crunched into the hangar wall. With vengeful eyes and faces hard as granite, the two of them turned their heads and watched Pasha and Annika disappearing out of sight in Karl's Audi SUV.

'Let's get out of here. The fire and police will be here soon,' said Danny, eyeing the plumes of black acrid smoke billowing from the burning hangar over the other side of the airfield.

'You get the spare, I'll jack the car up,' Valerik replied, his voice calm and cold as he walked towards Annika's Mercedes.

They worked fast, changing the shot-out tyre in record time, before reversing it out of the fence and accelerating away from the airfield.

'Pull in here,' Danny said, spotting a layby in the woods a couple of miles down the road.

Valerik did as Danny asked, parking up in the layby, leaving only a partial view of the road.

'What are we doing here?' Valerik said.

'Just wait a minute,' Danny said, nosing around the car while they waited.

He turned and spotted the butt of a rifle in the rear passenger footwell. When he pulled it out a Manila file slid out from underneath it. Danny put the rifle on the back seat and picked up the file. He opened it and frowned at photos of him, Tom and John clipped to MI6 papers and a classified order from Howard to collect information on a high-level storage facility north of Moscow.

'Come on, what are we waiting for? I want to get back to Moscow and kill that bitch,' said Valerik, gripping the steering wheel so tight his knuckles were turning white.

Danny pointed towards the road without lifting his head from the file. Twenty seconds later wailing sirens grew louder, shortly followed by a convoy of police and fire engines and ambulances moving at speed towards the airfield.

'Now we go,' Danny said, typing in a number before lifting Ivan's phone to his ear as Valerik drove out of the woods.

'Oxford Financial Consultants,' came the receptionist's voice.

'I need to talk to Howard,' said Danny bluntly.

'Stay on this number, Mr Pearson, he will contact you shortly,' the receptionist said, hanging up immediately.

CHAPTER 53

Frank pulled Howard's Audi Q7 to a halt outside his Whitehall HQ. He expected Howard to exit the car with his usual exuberant energy. When he didn't, Frank looked in the rear-view mirror at his boss. He was looking out the window, deep in thought. His face looked older than normal and the dark lines under his eyes were clearly visible.

'Are you ok, sir?' Frank said with genuine concern.

'Mmm, what? Sorry, Frank, I was miles away,' said Howard, sounding as tired as he looked.

'You look like you could do with a holiday, sir.'

'Yes, I think you could be right,' said Howard, finally getting out of the car.

'Shall I wait here, sir?'

'Er, no, Frank, I'll be some time,' he said before turning back. 'Take the rest of the day off. Here, be with your family, take them somewhere nice,' he continued, drawing the wallet out of his suit pocket. He slid a couple of fifty pound notes out and passed them to Frank.

'No sir, I couldn't possibly,' Frank protested.

'Please, take it.'

Frank looked at his tired boss. 'Thank you, sir,' he said.

Turning away, Howard entered the building. He'd only gone up a few steps when his phone buzzed with a message.

Daniel Pearson wishes to speak with you.

Frowning, Howard tapped the number attached to the message and put the phone to his ear as he continued up the stairs.

'Daniel, I assume by your call the three of you are not on the plane to Kiev I organised, at great cost I might add,' said Howard, his tone still upbeat.

'The airport was a trap, Volkov's men knew we were coming. Tom and John are dead,' Danny said coldly.

'I see. I'm very sorry to hear that. There's no way that information could have come from someone at your end?'

'None. There's more. Annika Volkov had a file on all of us, MI6 identifications and some bullshit orders with your name on to gain information on some facility north of Moscow,' said Danny angrily.

'Mmm, that does put a different light on things. I assume you don't want me to arrange an alternate evacuation plan for you?'

'Nope.'

'In that case, is there anything you need?'

'Yes, I'll send you a list,' said Danny bluntly.

'Ok, what about Tom and John's bodies?' said Howard, hating himself for having to ask.

'They won't be able to identify the bodies, they were burnt to ash with aviation fuel.'

The lack of emotion in Danny's voice told Howard he'd already gone into operation mode, pushing his emotion and pain into the deepest, darkest part of his brain, where the horrors of his past lived under lock and key.

'I'm sorry, they were good men. Send me that list,' said Howard with unaccustomed sadness in his voice. 'And Danny,' he added quickly.

'Yes.'

'Kill them all.'

'Roger that,' said Danny before hanging up.

Howard reached the top of the stairs, pausing as he reached out his hand to open the office door. A frown creased his forehead as he composed himself and pushed his way in.

'Boss, we've got a lead on the assets who…' said Martin, tailing off when Howard put his fingers to his lips.

As Brian turned in his seat, Howard put his fingers to his lips again and indicated for them to follow him back out of the office. Puzzled, they did as he asked and ended up on the landing.

'Brian, get a tech team to sweep the office for bugs, now, straight away, ok. Get the computers checked for viruses and spyware. We do nothing and say nothing in there until it's done,' said Howard, pausing as both men nodded their agreement.

'Martin, you said you had a lead on the assets. Have you said anything about that in the office?'

'Er, no, boss, the lead just came in from Mr Jenkins.'

'Good. I have some bad news to tell you. The extraction of our men in Russia was compromised. Annika Volkov's men were waiting for them, which resulted in Tomas Trent and John Ball's deaths. Daniel Pearson made it out ok and discovered forged documents that I can only assume were meant to be found with the bodies. These documents would have caused an international incident and would undoubtedly have resulted in the closure of this department, and the prosecution of myself. Now, as you know, our removal would mean the end of our current investigation, which would be rather convenient for our Minister of Defence, Mr Bullman. I think I speak for all of us when I say this one's personal. Let's bring our A-game, gentlemen. I want to nail this bastard to the wall,' Howard said to his two sombre looking analysts.

'Yes, boss. For William, Tom and John,' said Martin, with Brian nodding his agreement.

'Ok, let me know if the sweep finds anything. I'm off to see Edward and find out what he's got on the assets that killed William,' said Howard, managing a smile before he headed down the stairs.

He left the building, suddenly remembering he'd let Frank have the afternoon off. Undeterred, he walked down the narrow back road and cut through to Embankment, where he flagged down one of the numerous black cabs.

'Vauxhall Tube station, please,' Howard said. He didn't like to say the SIS or MI6 building that lay opposite theTube station. It invited too many questions.

'No problem, governor, I'll have you there in a jiffy,' said the cab driver, already diving into habitual small talk.

Howard smiled politely and answered the accustomed yes and no in all the right places, while inside, his mind was going to a dark place where decisions were made. Decisions over people living or dying.

CHAPTER 54

After a long car journey, Karl turned into the rebuilt Volkov estate. The men at the gates stood back and watched them drive through before closing them silently behind them. They resumed their uneventful sentry duty, yawning as they counted cars driving up and down the road outside.

'Wake up, you fucking idiots, you see anything suspicious you radio it in, ok?' growled Pasha, making them jump. 'Do you understand me?' he bellowed when they didn't respond quickly enough.

'Yes, Pasha, anything, we'll call it in,' the guard said nervously.

After fixing them with a ferocious stare, he turned and marched off after Annika who was storming into the house, her high heels clicking angrily on the marble floor.

She entered the large kitchen. Her face was calm and unexpressive once more, her ice-blue eyes telling another story as they burned furiously. 'Get out,' she said angrily to Karl and two men. When they didn't move immediately,

206

she noticed their eyes watching Pasha as he entered the room, waiting for his confirmation.

'What are you looking at him for? I said get out,' she shrieked.

The men still flicked their eyes back to Pasha, who jerked his head towards the door for them to leave.

'How dare you undermine me, here, in my own fucking home, Pasha,' Annika said, her voice back under cold control.

'I do not undermine you, Annika. You are a Volkov, the name, the figurehead. I am the power behind that name, the fear that enforces your word. I am not your bitch to bend to your every whim,' said Pasha, pacing around the kitchen unimpressed.

'I am Annika Volkov. You will do as I say,' she bit back.

Pasha turned to face her, his face contorting in anger. 'You think it's the name that brings you respect. This obsession with Pearson, the prison, the games and the failure. You have made us look like a laughing stock. Run Moscow? We can't even kill this one man. Your father would be turning in his grave,' he growled.

'I, I have to find him, family honour demands I kill him,' she said, Pasha's outburst making her feel like a child again. Memories of her father Yuri's outbursts that would send her crying to her room came flooding back.

'We do not need to find him. He is coming. He is coming to kill you, and when he does, I will be ready for him,' said Pasha, before walking out of the room.

Left alone in the white marble-topped kitchen, Annika's tough, ice-cold façade crumbled and she broke down, shaking uncontrollably, the tears cutting through her perfectly made-up face.

———

The car journey back to Moscow went by in silence. Both Danny and Valerik locked in tumbling thoughts as they moved from grieving and pain to revenge, death and destruction. Gradually both men pushed the loss of friends and loved ones to one side and filled the void with plans of revenge.

'So how are we going to kill this bitch?' Valerik eventually said.

'Well, we can't just rock up to the family estate. I'm sure there'll be a nice welcome committee waiting for us. No, we need to draw them out, divide and conquer. What businesses does she have in Moscow?'

'Plenty. Bars, whore houses, nightclubs, take your pick,' said Valerik, shrugging.

'The big ones?' Danny said.

'Ok, you've got a bar called Yuri's after her father, and a big nightclub called Diamonds. They also have a lap dancing club called Midnight. It's more of a whore house with rooms upstairs to serve the clients. Which one you want to hit?' said Valerik, the thought of positive action distracting him away from his father's and cousin's deaths.

'All three,' said Danny, deadly serious.

'All three!'

'In the same night,' Danny added.

'That sounds fucking crazy,' Valerik said, pausing for thought before adding, 'I'm in,' as a grin spread across his face.

'First we need somewhere to stay, then we need to check out the targets,' Danny said, texting clumsily on his phone.

'I have somewhere safe we can stay. What are you texting?' Valerik asked.

'A shopping list, just a shopping list,' said Danny, hitting send before smiling back at Valerik. His phone pinged with Howard's response within a minute.

Your request is noted. Sit tight. This may take a little time.

'Now I just need some food and a place to rest up for a bit,' said Danny, suddenly feeling drained after the day's events.

'No problem, we'll be there soon,' said Valerik as they hit the outskirts of the city.

Turning off the main roads, Valerik zigzagged through the city, making his way through the miles of bland-looking apartment blocks to the grandeur of the historical Old Arbat quarter of the city. Driving slowly down the narrow back streets, Valerik found a parking space alongside a heavily graffitied stretch of wall.

'Ok it's just round the corner,' said Valerik, getting out.

'Where are we going?' said Danny, folding the doctored file and tucking it in his jacket. He thought about taking the rifle but decided it was too hard to conceal and the last thing he wanted was police looking into gunman sightings.

'Natalya,' Valerik replied with a grin.

'Who's Natalya?' said Danny, following Valerik down a narrow alley.

'She's my, how you say, er, woman friend.'

'Girlfriend,' said Danny.

'Yeah, kind of.'

'When was the last time you saw her?'

'Er, about a year ago, we had a fight, and I stormed out. The police threw me in prison before we made up,' said Valerik, stopping by a heavy door with a row of buzzers next to it.

'You sure about this?' Danny said as Valerik pressed the buzzer.

'It's good, she's good girl, sometimes a bit, er, kaboom, yeah, but good girl,' said Valerik as a woman's voice said something in Russian over the intercom.

'Hey baby, it's me, Valerik. Let me in,' Valerik said softly back.

Danny raised his eyebrows as a never-ending stream of angry Russian profanities emanated out of the intercom.

'Come on, baby, it wasn't my fault. The Volkovs had me locked up in Lefortovo Prison. Let me in. I've missed you, honey. Come on, it's me, Valerik,' he said while Danny looked up and down the alley, wondering what they were talking about.

The conversation died, and they stood in tense silence for half a minute before the door lock buzzed open.

'You see, good girl,' said Valerik, pushing the door open with a big grin on his face.

CHAPTER 55

Up on the fourth floor of MI6's headquarters, or the SIS Building as it's commonly known, Howard knocked on the open door of the Chief of the Secret Intelligence Service Edward Jenkins's office. Edward looked up from his computer and frowned at Howard.

'Howard, are you ok? You look dreadful,' he said with genuine concern, beckoning him in.

'It's been a tough couple of weeks, my friend, and I fear I'm not getting any younger,' said Howard, trying to sound upbeat.

'Well, at least you can draw a line under Moscow; Danny and the guys will be back tomorrow,' Edward said with a smile.

'I'm afraid that will not be the case. They were ambushed at the airport. Tomas and John didn't make it.'

'Christ, and Daniel?' said Edward.

'Daniel is taking the loss very personally, as one would expect. I fear the less we know about his plans the better.'

'How did they know about the airport?'

'I have my suspicions, and if proved right, things could get rather messy. For that reason, I'd rather keep you out of this, Edward,' said Howard with a weary smile.

'I see. Does this have anything to do with a certain minister we have been looking into?' said Edward with a knowing look.

'What news have you got on the gentlemen who broke into my office and killed William?' Howard said, changing the subject.

Without pushing the point, Edward opened his desk drawer and passed a file over to Howard. 'Two possibles, two retired MoD assets in the capital at the time. One took a flight to Spain, the other a flight to Amsterdam hours after William was killed.'

'Thank you, Edward, I'll take it from here. Close the investigation into Mr Bullman and forget you ever saw this,' said Howard, taking the file and getting up to leave.

'As you wish. Look after yourself, Howard,' said Edward, watching him leave.

'Thank you, Edward, you've been a great friend to me,' Howard said with unexpected sentiment.

He made his way out of the office and passed through the usual security check before leaving the building. He was making his way to Vauxhall Tube station where he knew he'd pick up a cab, when his phone rang.

'Yes, Brian.'

'Hi, boss. We've just had the office swept and the computers checked. They're all clean, but we found a couple of listening devices,' said Brian.

'I suspected as much. Thank you, Brian, I'll be back shortly,' Howard said, hanging up.

He waved down an approaching cab and got in for the return journey to his Whitehall office. As it crawled its way through the heavy London traffic, his phone buzzed with a message from Lem Vassiliev.

The consignment will be ready tomorrow.
All debts are paid, my friend.
You are on your own. Good luck.

Howard smiled at the message. The world was a simpler place when he and Lem Vassiliev first met. Twenty minutes and a quick browse through the file Edward had given him later, Howard was once again climbing the steps to his office. Unlike earlier, the information from Edward, the message from Lem and the discovery of the office bugs had put a spring back in his step and chased the tiredness from his face.

'They're over there, boss,' said Brian, pointing to two tiny disconnected devices sitting on the desk.

'Thank you, Brian, I'll take care of them,' Howard said, picking them up and placing them into his jacket pocket.

'What do you want us to do next, boss?' said Brian.

'I want all of you working on the link between James Bullman and the Volkovs. I want you to go back as far as Viktor and Yuri Volkov's rise to power six, seven, eight years ago. Liaise with Edward; MI6 and MI5 had files on them back then. Look into the connection between Annika Volkov and Bullman, get Lionel to give his little street network a shake, give him some money from the special projects fund to loosen their tongues,' said Howard, checking his watch. 'On second thoughts, it's been a particularly awful day, gentlemen, and I think it would be best ended by raising a glass to absent friends. So if you would

213

STEPHEN TAYLOR

like to join me in the Silver Cross around the corner, I would like to buy you all drink,' said Howard with a smile.

The team went silent for a moment. They had worked for Howard for some time and although he was a fair boss, the line between work and private life had never been crossed.

'Lead the way, boss,' Brian finally said, prompting the others to follow.

214

CHAPTER 56

Valerik pushed his way through the apartment door, ducking immediately as a glass vase came flying his way. Danny's arm shot out with lightning reflexes as it passed over Valerik's head, catching the vase in his hand inches before it shattered on the wall. He placed it gently down on a small table by the door and stood silently as Natalya shouted angrily at Valerik.

'What the fuck, Val, you disappear a fucking year ago, nothing, not a word. What, you couldn't make a fucking phone call? And now you walk in here like nothing's happened.'

'Hey baby, it wasn't my fault. I left here and that bitch Volkov had her crooked fucking police grab me. I've been in Lefortovo Prison all this time. I'd still be there if this guy and my father hadn't got me and Leonid out,' said Valerik, looking at Natalya with sad, sorry eyes.

'What, you expect me to believe that shit? No, no, you can fuck off back to your father and that useless cousin of yours,' Natalya said, her anger waning a bit.

'I can't. We were ambushed by Volkov's men earlier

today. They killed my father, Leonid, Pyotr and his friends,' said Valerik in a low voice, pointing back at Danny.

Natalya looked at Valerik, his face loaded with grieving sadness and then at Danny's face, hard, his eyes distant, dark and dangerous.

'Swear you're not bullshitting me, Val,' she said, shocked by the news.

'I swear, baby, they're all gone, you're all I have left.'

She looked at him for a few seconds, all the anger leaving her as she moved forward and grabbed Valerik, embracing him as tears trickled down her cheeks. 'Oh, baby, I'm so sorry,' she said, placing her hands on his cheeks and kissing him passionately.

'God, I missed you,' said Valerik, kissing her back.

'What the fuck's his problem?' Natalya said, spying Danny over Valerik's shoulder still standing in the doorway, looking unimpressed.

'Oh, that's Danny, he's from England, he doesn't speak any Russian. Be nice, Natalya, I owe him my life,' said Valerik, kissing her again.

'Hey, come, sit, er, make comfortable,' Natalya said to Danny with her limited English.

Danny nodded and sat down, the grip of his gun becoming visible as his jacket flopped open. Natalya spotted it and felt inside Valerik's jacket, her hand recoiling at the touch of his gun.

'We've got to finish this, Natalya. It's the only way we can be free of the Volkovs and avenge my father's and Leonid's deaths.'

Natalya stood shocked for a moment then nodded her head. 'Ok, you do what you have to do,' she said, looking him in the eye.

Ivan's phone buzzed as Danny sat on the sofa. He didn't understand what Valerik and Natalya were saying to each other, but from the tone and body language, it seemed to be going well. He glanced at the message, then back to Valerik. 'The stuff will be ready tomorrow. We need to go and check out the targets tonight,' Danny said with little emotion.

'Ok, ok, let's have some food. Natalya, U tebya yest' yeda?' said Valerik, asking Natalya if she had any food.

'I can do some pirozhkis and shashliks,' she said, heading into the kitchen.

'Thank you, baby.'

Valerik sat down in the chair opposite Danny. His body seemed to disappear into it and his face looked tired and drawn.

'Are you ready for this, Valerik, because the odds aren't in our favour,' said Danny, looking over at him.

'I'm ready, my friend. The odds have been against me my whole life, yet here I am, still breathing.'

'You and me both,' Danny replied with a smile.

They ate and chatted, trying to keep the conversation light and away from recent events and things to come, for Natalya's sake. Danny borrowed Natalya's laptop while she and Valerik disappeared to the bedroom to get reacquainted. He Google Earthed Yuri's Bar, Diamonds and the lap dancing club called Midnight, making notes before checking all the venues on social media to get an idea of the internal layouts. Mentally blocking out noises he'd rather not hear from Natalya's bedroom, Danny studied the club's locations and all the routes and times it would take to cross from one venue to the other. When he'd found out all he could, he cemented it to memory and pages of notes. Moving on Danny searched to find out all he could on Annika Volkov and Pasha Manolov. He found a building registration for the rebuilding of the Volkov estate. He smiled as he thought of his computer genius friend

Scott Miller when Google Translate kicked in and changed it all to English. Further searching turned up precious little on the two names, which wasn't surprising given their background.

'Hey, what are you doing sitting around, you ready to go?' said Valerik, coming back into the small living room with a big grin on his face.

'Yeah. Everything's good between you and Natalya?' Danny said, returning the smile as he got up.

'Oh, yeah, real good, man. Come, she said we can borrow her car,' said Valerik, shaking a set of keys at Danny.

When they hit the street, Valerik pressed the button on the key and looked around. Three cars down, an ordinary-looking Lada Granta flashed its lights and unlocked.

'She didn't lend you her car, did she?' Danny said, shaking his head as he got into the passenger side.

'She might have done, if I'd asked her,' Valerik replied, getting in and starting it up. 'Where to first?'

'Yuri's Bar, it's the closest.'

After only a ten-minute drive, Valerik pulled the car over fifty metres down the road from Yuri's Bar. It was modern and bright with the name lit up in neon blue above the door. Danny and Valerik got out and walked past on the other side of the street.

'Two bouncers on the door, does it get rough in there?' asked Danny.

'No, everybody knows who owns it. You start trouble in there and Pasha would find you and fuck you up.'

'Good, so they won't have many bouncers inside.'

They carried on until they found an alley leading down the side of the bar, which gave access to the fire exit at the rear of the building.

'Ok, I've seen enough. Let's go,' Danny said, turning back up the alley.

'Ok, you're the boss,' said Valerik, following.

Timing them from the moment they left, Danny made some notes as they moved on to the nightclub Diamonds. They walked around the building as they had before until Danny had seen enough. Timing the journey again, they drove to the last stop, the lap dancing club Midnight.

'This one will be the hardest,' Danny said, looking at the imposing building with its neon signs and blacked-out windows.

'Yeah, why this any different?' asked Valerik.

'Lap dancers equal more girls, more touchy punters, more money, which all means more muscle looking after them. This will be the last place we hit.'

'Ok, how do we do that?' said Valerik, puzzled.

'Planning, Valerik, planning. But that's for tomorrow, it's been a long, shitty day and I need some sleep.'

'Yeah, I'll agree with that,' said Valerik, swinging the car around and heading back towards Natalya's.

CHAPTER 57

Larry Whistle yawned and powered down his
computer. He looked around the dark office.

The last one out again.

He stood up and pulled his jacket off the back of the
chair and slid it on. Working his way out of the high-secu-
rity building through several facial recognition-controlled
doors, Larry finally entered the lobby and headed to the
exit.

'Night, Bob,' he said to the security man on the desk.

'Yeah, night, Larry,' Bob said, pressing the door release
button on the desk to let him out. The late night air was
cool and the streets quiet as he strolled towards Trafalgar
Square and Charing Cross tube station. He looked both
ways to cross a road and noticed two men walking twenty
metres behind him. They were looking straight at him as
they walked, ominously dressed in dark jeans and dark
bomber jackets with identical crew cut hairstyles. Even
though he rationalised that they were just walking in the
same direction as him, he quickened his pace.

A little way on, Larry couldn't fight the urge to look

behind him any longer. His pulse raced and panic gripped him at the sight of the men only ten metres back, still staring straight at him, still relentlessly following. Larry started to run.

Just get to the Tube station. There'll be help there and I'll be safe.

He looked back again, terrified to see the two men jogging effortlessly after him, no panting, not even a bead of sweat trickling down their faces. Looking back where he was going, Larry jumped and stumbled to a halt as two clones of the men following appeared in front of him, while he stood frozen, like a rabbit caught in headlights.

A blue panel van pulled alongside them, its door already opening before it came to a halt. A hood was thrown over Larry's head and arms grabbed him from behind, pulling him inside, the door sliding shut behind him like he'd been swallowed by a wild animal. The van sped off and a Range Rover Sport instantly took its place. The four men got in and the car before it pulled away after the van.

———

Some time later the van stopped and Larry was led, shaking, into a building, his wrists zip-tied behind his back, the hood still firmly over his head. He heard the sound of a heavy metal door creaking open before he was pushed roughly inside. Hands forced him down into a hard chair and left him sitting there. Terrified beyond belief, Larry shook uncontrollably. Tears rolled down his cheeks under the hood as he sat, every minute feeling like an hour. After an eternity, the door creaked its way open and footsteps echoed, slow and deliberate, moving their way behind him, then circling in front. A chair was dragged across the floor in front of him, screeching slowly on the concrete floor. Then silence. Nerve-jangling minutes later, the hood was whisked off his head, leaving him struggling to focus in the harsh strip lighting. When the stars had cleared, a suited man was sitting cross-legged opposite him, picking a bit of lint from his suit trousers. Larry looked up at the man's face in surprise.

'Good evening, Mr Whistle. You know who I am so I'll dispense with the introductions. I've been told you're a smart man, so I'm sure you've figured out what this place is and what takes place here,' said Howard, pausing for effect as he watched Larry's eyes taking in the interrogation cell.

'Please, I haven't done anything,' Larry stammered, his eyes wide in fear.

'Now, now, Mr Whistle. We both know that's not entirely true, don't we?' said Howard, standing. He removed his jacket and placed it carefully on the back of his chair. Looking over Larry's head, he gave a curt nod, which was instantaneously followed by hands grabbing Larry's shoulders from behind.

'Mmm, it's been a while. Waterboarding has always been very effective, leaves no physical marks. I experienced it once, horrendous ordeal, I must say. You really do feel like you're drowning,' Howard said, watching Larry crumble into a blubbering wreck.

'No, please, I just do as I'm told. The Minister, Mr Bullman, gives the orders. He had your man Pearson tracked for the Russians and he ordered the surveillance on you and had your office bugged,' said Larry in tears.

Howard smiled at Larry. He placed his hands on the steel table between them and leaned in. 'I am fully aware of that little gem of information, Mr Whistle. What I would very much like to know is why our esteemed Minister of Defence is helping a lowlife Russian Mafia boss like Annika Volkov,' said Howard, standing up then reaching down behind the desk. 'Gentlemen,' he continued, bringing a bucket of water and a towel up.

The two men behind Larry picked him up off his feet and dumped him down on the steel table, face up.

'Pictures, she's had pictures of him and underage girls. He wanted me to destroy some files on his computer so they could never be traced, I wasn't supposed to look but I did. He likes to torture and rape young girls, I swear,' Larry screamed as the shadow of Howard holding the towel cut in front of the harsh strip lighting above him.

A nod from Howard and Larry was dragged off the table and slammed back in the chair.

'That wasn't too hard, was it, Mr Whistle?' said Howard, placing the bucket and towel behind the desk before sitting back down. He smiled at Larry, crossed his legs, and placed his hands in his lap. 'Now, about these young girls…'

CHAPTER 58

anny snatched the mobile phone up a split second after the message alert. It was only six in the morning, but he hadn't been sleeping. Thoughts of Leonid, Kristof, Tom and John haunted his usually clear mind.

White VW Transporter outside Burganov House Museum on Bol'shoy Afanas'yevskiy Pereulok, 15, ctp. 9, Moscow.

Key in magnetic box under driver's side wheel arch, requested items in the back. Good luck.

Opening Natalya's laptop, Danny googled where the location was. Seeing it was only a couple of miles away, he decided to go and get it. Throwing on his jacket and tucking the gun in the back of his jeans, Danny scribbled a note for Valerik, grabbed Natalya's door keys, and left the apartment.

The morning air was fresh, and the sun was just pulling

itself up above the horizon. The old part of the city was covered in tall, pristine buildings painted in a bright assortment of pinks, oranges, and yellows. Walking at a brisk pace, Danny turned into Bol'shoy Afanas'yevskiy Pereulok. He slowed to stroll, looking casually around, relaxed outwardly. Inwardly, he was tense and alert. His eyes scanned the road and pavements and cars, and at the same time he was subconsciously processing the buildings and windows in his peripheral vision for threats. He spotted the van opposite the museum and walked towards it. Without turning his head, he walked straight past and continued along the road, all the time scanning his surroundings. After going fifty metres down the road with nothing alerting his senses, Danny spun on his heels and walked back. Coming alongside the driver's side wheel, he bobbed down and felt under the wheel arch, thankful to feel the magnetic box. He pulled it off and opened it, pressing the unlock button on the key inside. Taking a final look around, Danny got in, started the van up and drove off, resisting the temptation to floor it in every gear out of there as soon as possible.

He took several detours, crossing the route he'd used to get there several times before he was satisfied he wasn't being followed, then headed back to Natalya's apartment. Driving a little way up from where they'd parked Annika's car the day before, Danny hopped out and went to the van's back doors. He checked nobody was around before opening up. Two large black canvas bags lay on the floor in the back. Danny turned the door light in the ceiling to on, then climbed inside, closing the back doors behind him. He unzipped each bag in turn, did a quick visual check, then zipped them back up again. Climbing back out, Danny pulled the bags towards him before heaving the straps over his shoulders one at a time. He shut the van's doors and headed up the alley to Natalya's apartment. By the time he dumped the bags down on the living room floor, his breathing was heavy and a trickle of sweat ran down his temple. He looked towards Natalya's bedroom door at the end of the corridor and then at his watch. Seven twenty and no one's stirring.

Turning his attention back to the canvas bags, Danny unzipped them and started pulling out the contents, placing them carefully on the carpeted floor. He was in the middle of cleaning and checking the last AK-74 assault rifle when Natalya came out of the bedroom, she froze in the hall at the sight of Danny sitting on the sofa holding a rifle surrounded by an armoury of guns, grenades, knives and body armour.

'Morning,' he said casually.

'Er, good morning,' she said before yelling for Valerik.

'Yeah, I'm coming,' Valerik said, plodding down the hall to join her. 'Fuck me.'

'Morning to you, too,' Danny said with a smile.

'What the hell is that?' Valerik said, looking at the rifle Danny was holding.

'This is an AK-74M assault rifle with optic sight and a GP-34 grenade launcher,' said Danny, spinning it around and handing it to him.

'And all this?' Valerik said, looking at the kit on the floor.

'Twelve 40-round magazines, six smoke grenades, four frag grenades, gas mask each, four Beretta 96 A1 handguns with three twelve-round magazines each and two silencers, two AUS-8 combat knives, two bulletproof tactical vests, oh and four bars of plastic explosives, detonators and timers.'

'Wow, I'm going to pump a grenade up that bitch's ass

and blow her fucking head off,' said Valerik, going through the motions with the rifle.

'You'll probably blow balls off. Now if you boys have finished comparing penis's, I will make breakfast, da,' said Natalya, walking into the kitchen unimpressed.

'She's got a point. I need to show you how to use this lot until you can do it blindfolded, and I need to go through the plan until it's second nature,' Danny said, taking the rifle back off Valerik.

'Ok, ok, we have breakfast then get to work.'

CHAPTER 59

Pasha stood out the front of the Volkov mansion. He stared at the front gate with dark, brooding eyes. The constant failure to kill Pearson was feeding his paranoia, making him conscious of every sideways look from his men. The sound of laughter made him snap his head round to the two men sharing a joke by the cars. Enraged, Pasha stormed over to them. He had his gun out and levelled at the man's laughing head before he could blink.

'You dare laugh at me. You think I'm a joke, eh? Is that what you think?' he yelled at the startled man.

'No, Pasha, I was not laughing at you. I would never laugh at you,' he said, turning as white as a sheet as he put his hands up passively.

'Hey, come on, Pasha, we weren't laughing at you,' said the other man, trying to calm Pasha down.

'Hey, hey, whoa, brother, come, calm down,' said Karl, hurrying over from the front gate.

Karl put his hand on top of Pasha's gun and gently put pressure on it until he lowered it down to his side.

'You two fuck off. Check the rear of the house, da,' Karl said hastily. The two men didn't need telling twice and scurried away.

'They were disrespecting me, I know it,' Pasha said, holstering his gun.

'No, they weren't. If they were, I would have put a bullet in their heads myself. Come, let's walk,' said Karl, nodding his head for Pasha to follow him around the gardens.

'Annika's obsession with this man has made us all look weak. If we do not end this soon, others will come to take everything away from us,' Pasha growled.

'Perhaps there may be something good to come out of this,' said Karl, his voice low, not to be overheard.

'Something good. What do you mean?' Pasha said, as the two of them moved further away from the mansion.

'Well, if this man Pearson were to kill Annika Volkov before you can kill him, you would be in the perfect place to take over Moscow. The men would follow you and the other Mafia families would be satisfied that revenge for Yuri and Annika had taken place. They would support your position as the boss.'

Pasha stopped in his tracks and stared at Karl for a minute. Even though he was Pasha's brother, Karl thought he'd overstepped the mark and Pasha was going to go for his gun.

'And how are we going to make sure that happens?' Pasha finally said, to Karl's relief.

'You said it yourself. Pearson will come. He knows he has to finish it or he'll spend a lifetime looking over his shoulder. We wait. When he shows, she dies. Who's to say if he did or didn't kill her?' said Karl, catching sight of Annika standing in the entrance to the mansion, shouting orders to some of the men as they approached.

229

Pasha's eyes focused on Annika like a wild animal spotting its prey, a small smile curling up in the corners of his mouth. 'I think you could be right, brother.'

'I am. It's our time to rule,' said Karl, splitting off from Pasha as he headed towards Annika.

'Pasha, have you heard anything? What's going on?' Annika said in her usual cold, demanding way.

'Don't worry, we are ready for him, you're going to get the revenge you deserve,' Pasha said, moving up beside her.

'Good, this has gone on long enough,' she said, spinning on her heels and clicking her way back into the house.

'It certainly has,' said Pasha under his breath.

CHAPTER 60

t was early afternoon and Danny had been transported back five years. He sat a hundred metres down from the rebuilt Volkov mansion, in the same parking space, in the same petrol station, eating another limp sandwich and drinking terrible coffee while checking out the mansion through its large, black, iron gates.

'I get the clubs, but how are we going to get past the gates and guards, they'll see us coming a mile off,' said Valerik, turning his nose up at the coffee.

'It's all about timing. We hit the first two clubs at the same time to draw them out. While they're dealing with that, we hit the lap dancing club and wait. All goes ok, they'll take us right inside,' said Danny, winding down the van window and chucking the rest of the coffee out.

'And if we get it wrong?' said Valerik, turning to look him in the face.

'Then we'll be dead and it won't matter anyway,' Danny said back with a smile.

'Shit, just another day in Moscow. Well, we have a few

hours to kill. What say we go to a bar and drink a toast to fallen friends and family before things get ugly?'

'Best thing you've said all day. We'll pick up Annika's car on the way,' said Danny, starting the van and turning back towards Moscow.

The two drove the rest of the way in silence, each lost in thoughts of what had recently happened and what they were about to do. Once they were back in Old Arbat, Danny cautiously drove past the place where they had parked Annika's car after the airport attack. Even though everything seemed as they had left it, Danny circled around the block and drove past in the opposite direction.

Nothing out of the ordinary; no one who doesn't fit in hanging around the streets.

On the third approach, he stopped to let Valerik out.

'Follow me, there's a place close to Yuri's Bar, it's quiet, tucked down a back street,' said Valerik, jumping into Annika's car and quickly driving it away ahead of Danny.

When they passed Yuri's, Danny slowed the white Transporter van. He took a long look at the building, photographing its daytime image to memory before following Valerik down a side street to a small traditional Russian bar, not more than two hundred metres away from Yuri's.

'Good choice,' said Danny, getting out of the van.

'Quiet, yeah. My father used to come here where I was a boy. I used to play pyramid game, er, is like your snooker but with white numbered balls,' said Valerik, his face dropping at the reminder of his father's death.

'Get the drinks in and you can show me,' Danny said, to distract him.

'We play for money,' said Valerik, cheering up.

'Of course,' Danny said, grinning.

They drank a toast to John, Tom, Kristof and Leonid,

and played for a couple of hours while day turned to night and the time for action got close.

'It's time,' said Danny, placing the cue gently down on the pyramid game table.

Valerik did the same and followed Danny outside, opening the boot of Annika's car while Danny fetched his canvas bag from the back of the van and put it in.

'Ok, you get ready in the back of the van, I'll take the car. When I'm in position, I'll call you, yeah? From that point on you keep the call open and earpiece in, you tell me what's going on and listen to my voice, ok?' Danny said, his entire body switching into operation mode, his eyes dark and alert and his face hard as granite.

'Ok, got it,' said Valerik, nodding.

'Don't worry, this is the easy bit. Cause mayhem then come and meet me at Midnight lap dancing club,' Danny said, moving in and embracing Valerik. He gave him a quick slap on the back before getting in the car and heading off.

After the short drive to Diamonds nightclub, Danny pulled up fifty metres short and got out. He grabbed the bag from the boot and put it on the back seat. Climbing in behind it, he closed the door. Concealed by the privacy glass, Danny unzipped the canvas bag and started kitting up. With the ammunition, grenades and a knife in the tactical vest, Danny chambered a round in his handgun and rifle, then climbed into the front between the seats. He slid his earpiece in and attached the throat mic, then hit Valerik's number before sliding the phone into his top pocket.

'Yeah, I'm still here,' Valerik answered.

'You all ready?'

'As I'll ever be.'

'Ok, remember, park on the opposite side of the street,

leave the keys in and engine running. You don't want to be fucking around with them when you pull out,' Danny said, starting the car.

'Will you hear me alright with the gas mask on?'

'Can you hear me?'

'Yeah.'

'Well, I'm wearing the mask now. The throat mic picks up what you're saying, ok?' said Danny through the gas mask.

'Hang on. I've got mine on now, you hear me?'

'Loud and clear. Right, tell me when you're opposite the bar.'

Danny moved up the fifty metres until he was opposite the nightclub entrance and stopped. He waited thirty seconds or so until Valerik's voice came back over the earpiece.

'I'm in place.'

'Ok, ready?'

'Yep.'

'Let's go.'

CHAPTER 61

Stepping out of the car, Danny started across the road towards the front of Diamonds and the clubbers waiting in an orderly line behind the roped-off entrance. A few looked at Danny, frozen in disbelief as he lifted his gas mask and shouted what he hoped was 'Get out of here!' in Russian before pulling the mask back down and swinging the assault rifle up.

'What the fuck was that, get your mother out here?' chuckled Valerik over Danny's earpiece.

'Well, it worked, they're running. Hit the smoke,' Danny said, pulling the trigger on the grenade launcher.

There was a pop like a cork leaving a champagne bottle, only a hundred times deeper, as the grenade launched over the screaming, running crowd and shattered the nightclub window, disappearing inside.

'Give it another one. Remember, it's the yellow cap,' said Danny, pulling his one out of the tactical vest and sliding it into the grenade launcher.

'Got it,' said Valerik as Danny turned and fired a second smoke grenade through the far window.

Within seconds, smoke was pouring out through both broken windows and clubbers and staff were coughing and screaming as they pushed their way out of the entrance door. Danny fired a few shots in the air to stop them congregating in the street like a herd of sheep following each other around for safety. Moving to the entrance doors as the flow of people exiting the club dwindled, Danny aimed up and let a blast of fire off at the club's illuminated sign. Sparks danced across its surface as the neon lighting exploded behind the glass front, all shattering into a million pieces before falling to the ground like glass rain.

'I'm going in, you ready?' said Danny, pausing a second to hear Valerik's reply.

'Da, I think they're all out now. I'm going in too,' came Valerik's response over people's panicked shouting.

The smoke swallowed him as he moved through the door at the back of the foyer. The smoke was starting to clear, giving him a hazy view of the deserted dance floor and bar beyond. He walked slowly, allowing his eyes to become accustomed to the gloom. A barrage of machine gun fire over his earpiece stopping him in his tracks.

'Valerik, you ok? Talk to me, mate,' said Danny, concerned.

'I'm good, just shooting up the bar.'

'Ok, keep focused, is the bar empty?'

'Yeah, they're all out.'

'Ok, put the frag grenade in, the red one, stand behind something for cover and fire it into the furthest corner,' said Danny, loading his grenade launcher as he leaned against a pillar.

Danny squeezed the trigger and launched the grenade at the DJ booth before he tucked himself back behind the pillar as it exploded in a fireball. Bits of grenade, decks and audio equipment ricocheting off the surrounding walls.

Being a larger venue than Yuri's Bar, Danny slid another frag grenade in and fired it at the bar, destroying it in a shower of glass and flaming alcohol.

'We're done. Let's bug out and meet at the rendezvous point.'

'I'm on my way,' came Valerik's voice.

With the smoke clearing, Danny slid the gas mask up onto the top of his head and made for the exit. As he pushed through the doors into the foyer, his rifle was pushed to one side, and a fist the size of a dinner plate hit him square in the face. He fell back, his vision blurring as his eyes watered. Caught off-guard and dazed by the blow, Danny lost his grip on the rifle. Going on pure gut reaction, Danny hit the floor and kicked up with all his might. His boot made contact with the groin of the giant blurry shape in front of him. Sitting up and shaking the fuzz out of his head, Danny remembered hearing the rifle clatter to the ground beside him. The mountain of a man staggered back, holding his balls with one hand while going for the gun in his shoulder holster with the other. In sync with the big guy, Danny reached across and pulled his handgun, both men fixing on their target and firing at the same time.

'Danny, Danny, talk to me. Danny,' shouted Valerik, hearing the grunts followed by gunshots over his earpiece as he drove towards Midnight.

Lying flat on his back, it took Danny a minute or so to register what had happened. He sat up, struggling against the pain in his chest. Looking down, he saw two slugs in the middle of his bulletproof tactical vest.

'I'm ok,' he gasped to Valerik.

Picking his rifle up as he got to his feet, Danny stepped over the massive dead Russian and pushed open the doors to the outside. He fired a few shots in the air to scatter any hangers on, then staggered to Annika's car and slid into the driver's seat. He took a few seconds to control his breathing against the pain in his bruised chest, then threw it into drive and floored it, speeding away from the club. Tucked in the shadows, one of the club's bouncers called a number as he watched Danny disappear into the distance.

'I'm on my way. I'll be about fifteen minutes,' Danny said, checking the mirror for anyone following.

CHAPTER 62

'What?' Pasha growled down the phone.

'It's Erik from Yuri's. The bar is gone, Pasha, somebody came in with grenades and smoke and machine guns. I didn't know w—'

'Shut up Erik, sit tight. We're on our way,' said Pasha, cutting him dead.

'Karl. Brother, where are you?' shouted Pasha, marching around the mansion, ignoring his phone ringing again.

'I'm here, what is it?' said Karl, appearing from one of the many rooms.

'Somebody's hit Yuri's. Erik says it's completely destroyed. It's him. Pearson. I know it's him. Get the men, we go,' said Pasha, infuriated at the caller phoning him again.

'What?' Pasha bellowed down the phone, turning away from Annika as she stormed down the stairs to find out what all the yelling was about.

'Karl, what's going on?' she demanded.

'It's Yuri's Bar, it's been destroyed. Pasha thinks it's the Englishman.'

'What? We must go. NOW!' she yelled, furious that the bar named after her father could be destroyed.

'No, me and Karl will go. It may be a trap to get you. That was Luka at Diamonds. They hit there too.'

She looked at Pasha, her eyes burning furiously behind her calm exterior. 'Ok, you go,' she finally said.

Pasha turned and headed out with Karl close behind. 'Nobody comes through this door but me,' he said to the two men outside.

They nodded and shut the heavy mansion door behind him, taking up their positions on either side, one with an AK-47; the other with a pump-action shotgun.

'Why didn't you let her come, brother? We could have killed her at Yuri's Bar or Diamonds,' said Karl quietly to Pasha.

'Too many people. We cannot afford to be seen. If the other families thought we had taken out one of their own, we would be as good as dead. It has to be here at the mansion,' said Pasha, waving the men over.

'What if he doesn't come here?' said Karl.

'He's coming, brother. I know this man, he won't stop, he's coming. Now, you take three men and go to Yuri's. I'll go to Diamonds,' said Pasha, pulling his gun out as he climbed into the passenger side of the car.

Karl got into the other car as more men climbed in, all armed to the teeth with rifles, shotguns and handguns.

'Come on, step on it,' Karl shouted, watching his brother heading off in front of him.

240

CHAPTER 63

Danny killed the lights on Annika's car and drove the last fifty metres in the dark before pulling up behind the parked van. The van door opened the second he'd stopped and Valerik hopped out, scooted over to the passenger side, and got in.

'You ok, what happened back there? Whoa shit,' said Valerik, noticing the shot mark in the front of Danny's tactical vest.

'I'm ok, hurts like hell, but I don't think it fractured any bones.'

'Should we go?' said Valerik, the reality of the situation knocking his confidence down a peg or two.

'Yeah, I'm good to go if you are,' said Danny, looking Valerik straight in the eye.

There was a brief pause before Valerik smiled back. 'Let's do it, for my father and your friends.'

Danny nodded, pulling two handguns out and placing them in his lap as he started the car.

'Ok, remember what I said. Go in with the rifle slung across your back, use the handguns to clear the place, they'll be easier to use in a confined space. See anyone with a gun, shoot first, anyone comes at you without a gun shoot them in the leg, ok? They might just be a customer and I don't want to murder innocent people. Once inside, we go upstairs and clear the place, I don't want any of the women or punters burning to death after we let the frag grenades off downstairs,' said Danny, still looking into Valerik's eyes, making sure he saw the acknowledgement of what he was saying.

'Yeah, ok I got it,' Valerik replied.

'Good, I'll go in front, you stay close and cover my back.'

Valerik nodded.

'Ok let's go, we all gotta die sometime, right?' said Danny, moving out and heading towards Midnight lap dancing club a couple of hundred metres up the road.

He pulled up fast outside the entrance, his door opening and hands on his guns a second later. It was obvious the doormen had been alerted to the attacks on Yuri's and Diamonds, they were pulling guns out of their suit jackets the second they clapped eyes on Danny and Valerik.

His senses heightened Danny moved with intense focus. He double-tapped the triggers of both guns simultaneously, the close range blowing the doormen back off their feet as the bullets hit them in the centre of the chests. Without breaking his stride, Danny pushed through the entrance doors into a foyer with a cloakroom and a ticket booth. The women in the booth and cloakroom shrieked at the sound of gunfire and the sight of dead doorman lying outside. Danny put his finger to his lips to silence them, then turned to push the door to the club open. As he did, the coats in the cloakroom flew to one side and a heavyset Russian with cauliflower ears and a flattened nose burst through. His gun aimed at Danny's head. There were two loud bangs as Valerik pulled his trigger, knocking the man back into the coats in a cloud of red mist and brain matter. Danny whipped his head back to see what had happened and got a nod from Valerik. Nodding back, he turned back and entered the club.

The gunshots had already stopped activities inside. Suited businessmen and party revellers tore their eyes away from the semi-naked pole dancers still holding on to their poles fixed into the raised stages. Danny side-swiped one of the customers in the side of the head before letting off a volley of shots into the ceiling, while Valerik yelled at them to get out in Russian. After a second of shocked, delayed reaction, the crowd rushed forward and made a mass exodus for the exit, parting like a river round either side of Valerik and Danny. Gunshots sounded from the far side of the club as the crowd thinned. A customer and one of the dancers dropped like a stone to the floor beside Danny. Ducking down, he moved behind a seating booth while Valerik flattened himself behind a pillar. Looking between the running people, Danny focused on the view beyond, eventually picking out one of Volkov's men peeking over the bar, and another tucked down by the far edge of the stage.

'Valerik, behind the bar,' Danny yelled over the screams of the last few to leave.

'Ok,' Valerik shouted back, sliding his back down the pillar before moving low to the far end of the bar.

Crouched below the top of the it, Valerik looked across, waiting for instruction. Danny stuck up three fingers to signal go on three, then counted Valerik in. One finger, then two, then three. On the third, Valerik swung his arms up, banging the butt of his guns down on the bar top as he popped his head up and looked along the sights into the serving area and Volkov's man crouching at the other end. As he pulled the triggers, Danny hopped up on the stage and exploded into a sprint while Volkov's second man tried to get a shot across at Valerik.

By the time he realised Danny was coming at him, it was too late. He started moving his gun in Danny's direction but only got halfway before Danny kicked him in the head at full speed, like a footballer taking a penalty. The blow whipped the man's head unnaturally to one side before his body followed it to the floor. On the other side, the guy behind the bar slumped to the floor. Valerik stood and moved across to join Danny as he jumped down from the stage and looked at his watch.

'Six minutes. Someone will have called Annika by now. If they are at Yuri's or Diamonds, which I expect they will be by now, they'll be here in twelve to fifteen minutes,' Danny said moving to the stairs and the upper bedrooms. 'We've got ten minutes to clear everyone out and trash the place.'

CHAPTER 64

'All this was just the one man?' Pasha said, questioning one of the doormen while looking at the flames licking out of the window of Diamonds, and the other doorman dead on the floor with a bullet hole in his chest.

'Yes, it all happened so quickly. There were smoke grenades and automatic fire, then there were two big explosions, and he was gone,' said Luka, nervously avoiding Pasha's angry stare.

'Pasha, Pasha,' came a shout from one of the men by the car.

'What is it?'

'They're hitting Midnight. They're there now, right now,' he shouted.

'Get in the car, NOW!' Pasha yelled, pulling his phone out to call his brother. 'Karl, get to Midnight as quick as possible. What? Yes, they are there now,' he said, the car already moving as he pulled the door shut.

———

'Is that the last?' Danny said, watching a semi-naked businessman and lap dancer-cum-prostitute, clatter down the stairs.

'That's it,' said Valerik, appearing from the bedroom.

'Ok, let's get out of here,' Danny said, looking at his watch as they moved down the stairs.

Entering the main part of the club, Danny and Valerik swung their rifles up and emptied the magazines at the bar. Moving to the exit, Danny turned and fired a frag grenade at the stage while Valerik fired one into the bar. Wood, glass, and liquor flamed and blew across the club. When the explosion died down, they threw their rifles down and pulled out their handguns. Ejecting the empty magazines, they slid in fresh ones from their tactical vests. Holstering one so he could attach a silencer to the other, Danny waited for Valerik to do the same. While checking his AUS-8 combat knife was in its sheath, he looked at his watch again.

'Ok, let's go. They'll be here any minute now,' said Danny, pushing the door open to look out at Annika's car.

———

'Come on, move it!' Pasha yelled, gripping the door handle as the driver slid the car sideways around a corner.

The car snaked down the damp road before straightening up and hurtling towards Midnight club. As they got closer, they could see black acrid smoke rising above neighbouring buildings before the club itself came into view. Guns at the ready, the car skidded to a halt and the men poured out onto the empty road. At the sound of a revving car, they all turned, fingers hovering over their triggers, only relaxing when Karl and his men skidded to a halt beside them.

'Argh, that fucking Englishman,' Pasha yelled, noticing Annika's car parked outside the entrance, its front doors open, keys still in the ignition and engine still ticking over.

He walked cautiously over with his gun up, and ducked his head in with his gun pointed into the back seats. All clear. As he backed out, he noticed a file on the passenger seat. Reaching in, he grabbed it and opened it to find pictures of the Volkov mansion and floor plans of its interior.

'Shit, it's a diversion, he's going for the mansion. Everyone get back there now. Karl, get in, we'll take Annika's car, come, hurry,' Pasha yelled, climbing into the driver's seat.

Karl ran over and got in the passenger seat, while the other cars floored it, their tyres spinning and fighting for grip as they sped away towards the Volkov mansion.

With the phone jammed under his chin as he drove, Pasha called the men on the gate at the mansion.

'It's Pasha. The Englishman is coming after Annika. Get everyone covering the perimeter wall and gates, ok?, It's the only way he can get in. I'll be back in ten minutes.'

'How can he get in through all of us?' said Karl, sitting calmly in the passenger seat.

'I don't know, but he must have planned for it somehow. When he does, we will take care of him and Annika.'

'Mmm, the Manolov brothers running Moscow at last. I like the sound of that,' Karl said with a grin.

'Don't underestimate the Englishman Karl, he's like a cat with nine lives,' said Pasha, shooting him a warning look.

'Bah, he's just a man. I'll put a bullet in his head. He dies like all the rest.'

CHAPTER 65

The guards rushed to open the iron gates as the cars approached, shutting them again as soon as the last one had driven through. They turned around the ornate fountain and reversed up to park in a line in front of the mansion.

'Anything?' Pasha shouted as he got out of the car.

'No, nothing.'

'Ok, keep your eyes open and call me if you see anything,' Pasha said, turning to the men as they got out of the cars. 'You two stay on the entrance, the rest of you watch the perimeter. Karl, inside with me.'

They headed inside, ignoring the two men in the hall as they made their way to the kitchen. The minute they entered, Annika's demanding voice could be heard as she descended the stairs to find them.

'Well, what is happening? Do my own men not report to me anymore?' she said, her voice raised and eyes darting angrily between Pasha and Karl.

'The Englishman and Valerik Turgenev have destroyed Yuri's, Diamonds and Midnight, and are coming here to kill you,' Pasha said bluntly while Karl moved away to the far side of the kitchen.

'Am I surrounded by idiots? You're telling me all of you cannot stop one single Englishman and that street rat Turgenev,' she said angrily as Pasha stood unimpressed by her outcry.

'Have you finished? I have had enough of your whining. You're a disgrace to the Volkov name. Your father was a great man, and it saddens me that you should die such a failure,' said Pasha, his eyes flicking over Annika's shoulder.

'How dare you, you are nothing without me Pasha, I—'

Her mouth froze mid-sentence and her body quivered. Her piercing blue eyes went wide before losing their shine. She flopped onto the kitchen's marble worktop like a piece of meat slapped onto a butcher's block, leaving Karl standing behind her, blood dripping from a long hunting knife.

'No going back now, brother,' he said to Pasha.

———

'Ok, time to go,' whispered Danny, releasing his grip on the inside of the boot of Annika's car.

He popped it up out of the latch he'd broken earlier and looked through the crack at the bottom. Pausing a second until his eyes adjusted to the light, Danny couldn't see anyone directly behind them. He opened the boot wider and stuck his head out. To the left lay the corner of the mansion and the estate wall beyond. Two of Volkov's men, armed with rifles, appeared from the side of the building. They looked aimlessly up and down as they passed by and out of sight, their focus on an attack from outside of the wall. Turning his head the other way, Danny followed the front of the mansion towards the front door, which was obscured by Karl's car parked beside them.

'All clear.'

'Good, I need to get out of this fucking boot,' Valerik grumbled.

Gun in hand, Danny slid one leg out, then the other until he was crouched with his back against the car's bumper. Valerik did the same and covered left while Danny poked his head around the side of the car, looking towards the front gates. As he'd suspected, most of Volkov's men were milling around the outside of the estate, their attention focused outward rather than inwards. Tucking back in, Danny leaned forward just far enough to see the front door and the two guards chatting in front of it.

Taking a bar of plastic explosive out of his tactical vest, Danny set the timer to five minutes and popped it into the boot of Annika's car, shutting it down behind him.

'Ok stay close. I'll take these two out quick and quiet. When the car goes up, it'll keep them busy out here while we find Annika,' Danny whispered, taking the combat knife out of its sheath.

Valerik nodded and stuck close behind Danny as he leaned forward again to look at his targets. He tensed his legs, feeling the grip on the gravel under his feet, his eyes hawklike in the dark, watching for the right moment. The nearest guard turned his back to Danny as he continued his conversation, the move obscuring his colleague's view. At the same moment, Danny took off like a sprinter off the starting blocks. He covered the ten metres in a second, swinging his arm around the nearest guard and severing his windpipe with the knife. As the man dropped, clutching his neck in a futile attempt to keep the blood in, Danny popped off a silenced round into the forehead of the other guard, catching him as he fell, a stunned look locked on his dead face.

By the time Valerik caught up, Danny was already dragging the man out of sight behind Karl's car. Copying, Valerik dragged the second man back and crouched behind the car with Danny. No shouts, no gunshots. They still had the element of surprise.

Moving back to the door, Danny stood to one side and indicated for Valerik to knock. When the door started to open, Danny shoulder charged it with all his might, sending it crashing into the face of the guard behind. Watching his friend fall flat on the hall floor, the second man went for his gun, but he was too slow. Danny jammed the end of his silencer into the centre of the chest and squeezed the trigger twice. Stepping in beside Danny, Valerik shot the other man as he looked up from the floor, blood pouring from his nose as he opened his mouth to shout the alarm. Hastily shutting the front door, Danny bolted it and turned. As blood spread its way across the white marble floor, Danny and Valerik stood silent, guns up as they listened. The house was quiet. No one came rushing in to kill them.

Moving again, Danny took two bars of plastic explosive out of the vest and stuck one on the back of the front door. He checked his watch and set the timer for three minutes, then stuck the other bar on the structural wall under the sweeping marble staircase, setting the timer for four minutes.

'Let's go,' he said, leaving a bloody trail of footprints as he headed for the lounge.

CHAPTER 66

The plastic explosive went off in Annika's car with an ear-shattering boom as the blast ripped the bodywork apart like a peeled banana, before shredding the fuel tank and engulfing the wreck in a huge fireball that sprayed the neighbouring cars with spurts of burning fuel, igniting their interiors through the blown-in windows.

'What the fuck was that?' said Karl, jumping at the explosion and the mansion's front windows imploding from the shockwave.

'He's here,' said Pasha, drawing his gun.

Indicating for Karl to go through the door to the utility room, Pasha headed towards the door at the far end of the large kitchen.

Nodding, Karl drew his gun, and moved silently away.

Outside, Volkov's men ran towards the mansion, jumping away from the flaming cars as another fuel tank exploded. They tried the front door, hammering and shouting when they found it bolted shut.

'Pasha, Karl, is everything alright in there, is Miss

Volkov safe?' came the cry between the thumps on the front door.

Karl peeped round the side door from the utility room into the entrance hall. He couldn't see the front door around the stairs but spotted the bloody footprints leading to the lounge. He edged forward with his gun up, treading carefully, when the two dead guards on the floor came into view. Stepping over them, he headed for the front door to let the men in. A small square object stuck to the back of the it caught his attention. He stared at it for a few seconds before realising what it was. As the timer's little red digits counted down 5...4...3, Karl backtracked as fast as he could, slipping on the blood spreading across the shiny marble floor. He managed to duck behind the grand marble staircase a second before the device exploded, shredding the heavy oak door and sending hundreds of shards of wood outwards like mini spears, ripping the men outside to pieces.

When the explosion died down, Karl stepped back out, brushing the dust and debris off him as he stood looking at the gaping hole where the door had been. Trying to think through the ringing in his ears, he turned to go towards the kitchen, freezing at the sight of the second explosive device on the wall ahead of him.

'Bastards,' he said as the timer clicked down to zero.

The explosion blew Karl back off his feet as it ripped a large section of the supporting wall out, bringing the heavy marble staircase and landing crashing down, burying Karl in a torrent of dust and wood and marble debris.

Valerik jumped and twitched at the explosions as he followed Danny along a corridor at the rear of the house. In contrast, Danny was calm and focused. Every nerve and sense worked on what was ahead of him. Reaching the end of the corridor, he could see the kitchen through the partially open door in front of them. Darting his head forward for a quick look, Danny took in as much of the room as possible and didn't register any threats. He eased the door open and moved through, targeting his gun when he saw Annika Volkov sitting in a chair behind the kitchen island. She had a pale, waxy look about her as she stared back at him with striking blue, unblinking eyes. When Valerik came in behind him, he saw Annika and instantly moved his gun around to shoot her. Danny shot his hand out and grabbed Valerik's wrist.

'No point. She's already dead,' he said, letting Valerik go once the words had sunk in.

'What, no, what the hell's going on?' said Valerik, moving up beside Annika's dead body.

She was carefully balanced upright in the chair, a crimson stripe of blood down the back of her white Versace dress.

'Doesn't matter, it's done. We need to get out of here,' Danny said, unemotional, already dismissing the scene and moving on to his exit plan.

Valerik was about to say something when the door at the far end of the kitchen flew open. Pasha came charging out with a gun in each hand. Danny instinctively ducked behind the kitchen island as Pasha unloaded both weapons across the room, hitting Valerik in the chest and arm before thudding into Annika's body, forcing it to topple off the chair and land with a slap on the marble floor next to Danny. Out of bullets, Pasha slid to the floor on the opposite side of the kitchen island to reload. Ten feet of marble and wood away, Danny grabbed Valerik by the tactical vest and dragged him close.

'Valerik, stay with me, buddy,' he said, checking him over for wounds.

'Argh, fuck that hurts,' Valerik cried as he came to.

'You'll live. The vest caught most of it. Put pressure on the wound in your arm,' Danny said, aware of the sound of Pasha ejecting his empty magazines and clicking new ones into place.

Pulling the cupboards open behind him Danny pulled a stainless steel frying pan out and held it up over the marble worktop, angling it so he could see the other side of the island in its reflection. He caught a glimpse of Pasha as he aimed over the marble and shot the pan out of his hand.

Shit, this is taking too long. I've gotta get out of here.

CHAPTER 67

Danny looked up at the cut crystal glass chandelier hanging from the ceiling above Pasha's side of the island. He drew his other gun and aimed both weapons at the chandelier's fixings. With controlled squeezes he fired one gun after the other, chipping lumps of plastered ceiling until the fixing gave way and fell towards Pasha. With no time to get out of the way, Pasha had to drop his guns to catch the heavy chandelier. At the same time, Danny leaped up onto the marble worktop and jumped forward to loom over Pasha as he hurled the chandelier to one side. Pulling the trigger without a second thought, Danny's forehead creased when it clicked empty.

Before he could reload, Pasha shot his hands up and grabbed Danny's legs, whisking them from him. Danny fell back, smacking his shoulders and the back of his head on the unforgiving marble. Fighting dizziness and pain, he got his hands up just in time to block Pasha's barrage of punches; good punches, powerful and well placed, from a man who knew how to fight. Danny fell back on his mixed martial arts training and kicked Pasha back with a well-placed boot to his groin. Straightening up, Pasha pulled a six-inch hunting knife from a sheath on his belt. Placing his feet on the floor, Danny stood by the kitchen island and pulled the AUS-8 combat knife out, standing ready, his eyes locked and alert. The seconds felt like hours, both men building for the attack that only one of them would walk away from.

In a flash, Pasha lunged forward, slashing his knife to miss Danny's belly by millimetres as he jumped back. Noting Pasha's stance as he attacked, Danny moved the opposite way when he came in for a second attack, and powered a knee into Pasha's side as his blade fell short of its target. The blow threw Pasha off balance allowing Danny to grab his wrist and punch his own knife into Pasha's abdomen. The big Russian froze, deflated, as the air knocked out of him. He stared in a mixture of anger and disbelief. Staring back at him with dark, revengeful eyes, Danny twisted the knife and pulled it upwards into Pasha's heart. They stood there, locked in position for a few seconds, before Pasha crumpled and fell to the floor. Leaving the knife in him, Danny picked up his gun, loaded a full magazine, and moved around the island to help Valerik to his feet.

'You ok?'

'Yeah, I think so,' said Valerik, taking his hand off so Danny could see the wound.

'Looks like it went through the flesh, the blood's not pumping out so I don't think it's hit an artery. Come on, let's get the fuck out of here,' Danny said, putting Valerik's hand back on the wound.

Moving away, Danny turned on the gas to the cooker hob and oven before slapping the last bar of plastic explosive from his tactical vest on the hob. He set the timer for one minute, then scooted over to Valerik. Raising his gun, he shot the glass out of the large bifold doors leading to the back garden. Moving ahead of Valerik, Danny stepped out into the cold night air. A couple of poorly aimed shots whizzed passed him from the far corner of the mansion. Danny emptied a magazine in their direction, reloaded and kept his aim as Valerik joined him.

'That'll keep their heads down. Come on, we've gotta move,' Danny said, covering Valerik as they ran across the perfectly manicured lawn for the wall at the back of the estate.

By this time guards from the front had built up enough nerve to enter through the hole where the front door had been. When they saw Annika and Pasha's bodies, they rushed to the glassless door to see Danny and Valerik making their escape.

Taking aim with shotguns and rifles, they were a split second away from cutting them down when the timer on the hob clicked to zero. The plastic exploded in a fireball of ignited gas, flying lumps of cooker and pieces of marble worktop. While Volkov's men were killed or maimed or ran into the garden like flaming torches, Danny gave Valerik a leg up the wall, then pulled himself up and over the other side.

With the feeling of déjà vu, Danny helped Valerik across the field he'd crossed five years earlier. They reached Natalya's Lada Granta parked behind the same storage barn he'd parked his van behind when he'd killed Yuri Volkov. Finding one of Natalya's scarves on the back seat, Danny tied it tightly around Valerik's arm to stem the bleeding. His adrenaline was dropping and he was shaking as the shock of being shot set in, but he'd be ok. Reversing the little car onto the road, Danny drove back onto the main road. He turned past the front of the Volkov mansion, the guards out the front were shouting down their phones in a state of helplessness as smoke and flames took hold of the newly built Volkov mansion.

'We're in big trouble now,' said Valerik through chattering teeth.

'Eh, what? How do you figure that?' Danny said, looking across at Valerik, puzzled.

'We've got blood all over Natalya's car. She's going to kill us for sure,' Valerik said, managing a shaky grin.

CHAPTER 68

When they arrived back at Natalya's, she'd been too concerned about Valerik to worry about her car. Danny cleaned his wound while he downed the best part of a bottle of vodka to kill the pain. When the alcohol had taken effect, Valerik bit down on a folded towel, while Natalya held his arm and Danny sewed up the entry and exit wounds, ignoring his muffled shouts. Exhausted, stitched and bandaged up, Natalya put Valerik to bed. She came back through to the lounge a few minutes later and sat in the chair opposite Danny.

'Thank you for all you have done for Valerik. He's a shit, but I love him,' she said with a tear in her eye.

Caught off guard by the unexpected emotion, Danny just nodded.

'Ok, make yourself comfortable, good night,' she said, getting up and heading to the bedroom.

With all the mental stress and adrenaline long gone, tiredness hit him like a ton of bricks. He lay down on the sofa and was asleep moments later.

———

Something in his subconscious screamed at him to wake up. He didn't hear anyone straight away, just had a sense they were there. Lying there with his eyes shut, he heard their breathing from the chair opposite. It wasn't Natalya, her breathing was light and quick; it wasn't Valerik, Danny would have heard him coming a mile off. Whoever it was didn't want him dead, or he'd be dead. Snapping his eyes open, he fixed and focused on a suited, silver-haired man with classic Russian features and piercing sky-blue eyes that stared back at him intently.

'Mr Pearson, nice to meet you in the flesh, although I'm surprised to catch you with your guard down,' said Lem Vassiliev with a big grin.

Pulling down the blanket covering him, Danny revealed a Beretta handgun pointed directly at Lem's head.

'I stand corrected, you do live up to your reputation,' Lem said, still smiling.

'Fascinating as this is, would you mind telling me who you are and what the fuck you want?' Danny said, sitting slowly upright, his gun still trained on Lem's head.

'To the point, as always. Who I am is not important. Let's just say I am an old acquaintance of your boss and a friend of Kristof Turgenev. As for what I want, I am the bearer of good news, Mr Pearson. After reports of last night's excitement spread through Moscow, certain individuals have found themselves, er, shall we say, unemployed and considerably more talkative than they were yesterday. The result has been a number of arrests, including Moscow's police commissioner and the governor of Lefortovo Prison.'

'And I want to know this why?' said Danny impatiently.

'My apologies. I'll get to the point. You want to know

this because it means Mr Turgenev and yourself are no longer wanted by Russian authorities,' said Lem, standing up to leave. 'You are a free man, Mr Pearson, go home,' Lem said, getting up to leave.

'Were,' Danny said.

'Were what?'

'You were a friend of Kristof. He was killed, along with my friends at Novinka Airfield,' Danny said quietly.

'Am a friend, Mr Pearson. He and your friend Tomas Trent got out of the fire exit at the back of the hangar just before it went up. They are in the hospital with minor burns,' said Lem, opening the door.

Danny sat for a second, lost for words.

'Give my regards to Howard, Mr Pearson,' Lem said, closing the door behind him.

Letting out a sigh, Danny put the gun down on the table in front of him and wandered to the bedroom door. Natalya opened it when he knocked. Valerik was still sleeping, so he told her the news and went back to the kitchen to make himself a coffee. An hour or so later, he heard Valerik shouting in Russian and crashing about as he tried to get dressed with his arm in a sling.

'Danny, is it true? My father's alive,' he yelled, bursting out of the bedroom.

'That's what the Russian suit said, him and Tom are in the hospital.'

'We must go now. What did this guy look like?'

'Suited, short grey hair, stocky with really blue eyes. He said he was a friend of your father's,' Danny said shrugging.

'Sounds like Lem Vassiliev. He's a Secret Service man. My father used to do some work for him, like your Howard. Now we go, Natalya. I need to borrow your car again,' Valerik said excitedly.

'Ok, but you clean it up before you bring it back, I mean it,' she said, throwing Danny the key.

'Why didn't you give me the key, don't you trust me?' Valerik said with a grin.

'You can't drive with your arm in a sling, you idiot, and no, I don't trust you. I love you, but I don't trust you,' she said, wrapping her arms around him and giving him a kiss.

An hour later, they entered the hospital. Danny stood by as Valerik talked with receptionist to find out where Kristof and Tom were. Danny took the stairs while Valerik shook his head and took the lift to the fourth floor ward. Valerik found Kristof with bandages on one arm and both hands, but apart from that, he seemed to be in good spirits.

'Good to see you alive,' Danny said to Kristof.

'Thank you for all you have done. We are forever in your debt,' Kristof said, with a look that said he meant it.

Danny just nodded and left them jabbering away in Russian while he went to find Tom. He was lying in a bed by the window, looking bored. He had bandages on his left leg and left hand but otherwise looked ok.

'About time you turned up, I can't understand a fucking word anyone says around here,' said Tom, grinning.

'Sorry, I'll try to be a bit quicker next time,' Danny said, taking a seat beside him.

'Seriously, it's good to see you, mate. I didn't know you were still alive until I saw the news about Volkov's death and the destruction of the mansion this morning. It had you written all over it,' Tom said with a chuckle.

'The others didn't make it then,' said Danny, turning serious.

'No, I'm afraid not.'

'When can you get out of here?' Danny said, changing the subject.

'The doctor said in a couple of days.'

'Ok, you rest up. I'll talk to Howard and get the flights home booked.'

'Sounds good to me. The sooner I get out of Russia the better.'

'I'll second that, mate,' Danny said, smiling.

CHAPTER 69

Taking a while for his sleepy brain to register what had woken him, James Bullman sat upright in bed. The banging and shouting coming from the front door didn't let up and bright blue strobing lights danced from behind the curtains and flickered across the bedroom ceiling.

'What the blazes is going on?' James said out loud, turning the bedside light on and kicking his feet into his leather slippers. He threw on his dressing gown and went out onto the landing.

'Mr Bullman, could you come to the door, please?' came more shouts from outside in between the hammering on his front door.

What the bloody hell? Must be an attack or a defence crisis or something.

'Hang on, hang on, I'm coming,' he shouted, stomping down the stairs.

When he got to the bottom step, he noticed a glow across the mosaic tiled hall floor from under his office door. James froze. He was not a man to forget things, and he knew for certain he hadn't left the office light on. Tentatively, he placed his hand on the door handle and turned it slowly. Pushing the door an inch at a time, he opened it and peered inside. The light came from the lamp on his desk, its glare making the far side of his desk and the room difficult to see clearly. It did illuminate the top of the desk itself, and a small pile of files and photos spread all across the top that sent a shiver down his spine. He entered the office and slumped down in his old leather chair and looked at the pictures of him and young girls tied, chained, beaten and gagged as he performed various sex acts on them.

'Mr Bullman, sir, it's the police. Please open the door or we will be forced to break it down,' came more shouts and hammering from the front door. The noise made him look up from the pictures. His heart leaped and he jumped back in the seat at the sight of the asset he'd used to break into Howard's office sitting in the chair opposite, his eyes glazed and open in a deathly stare, a single bullet hole in the middle of his forehead. Standing up and backing away from the desk, he saw the second asset lying on the floor on his front, two bullet holes in the middle of his back. Dizzy with shock, James placed his hand on the desk to steady himself. The photo under his hand curled around a hard object underneath. Sliding the photo to one side, his Smith & Wesson M&P 9 handgun sat next to a small plastic box.

'Mr Bullman, this is your last chance to open the door. Mr Bullman? Right, boys, get the battering ram,' came the voice from the front door again.

James didn't hear them. He picked up the gun. The pungent smell of nitroglycerin confirmed his fears. It was his gun, with his fingerprints that had been used to kill the assets. Putting the gun back down, James picked up the small plastic box in his shaking hands. He opened it, dropping the box onto the desk at the sight of the two bugs from Howard's office. Slumping back into the chair, James looked at the surrounding scene: the photos, the dead men, his gun and the bugs. As the heavy battering ram crashed into the front door, splitting the frame before it burst open, James picked up the gun, placed it in his mouth and pulled the trigger.

CHAPTER 70

Pulling into his reserved parking place at Greenwood Security, Danny hopped out of his car and walked to the front of the building. He leaped up the stairs in his usual three-at-a-time sprint, pushing the squeaky old oak office doors open at the top.

'Morning, Lucy, is the boss in?' he said to the receptionist on the desk.

'Yes, he has someone in with him at the moment.'

'Thank you, Lucy,' Danny said over his shoulder.

'Good to have you back,' she added a little eagerly.

'Good to be back, Lucy.'

As he made his way to his office with its sign on the door: Danny Pearson, Director of Operations, he glanced across at his boss and friend Paul Greenwood's glass-walled office. He recognised the size and shape of Paul's suited visitor instantly as Howard. Catching Danny looking through the glass, Paul beckoned him in.

'Paul, Howard,' Danny said, nodding to the two of them.

'I'm afraid you're mistaken, dear boy, the name's David Tremain,' Howard said with a smile.

'Mr Tremain here is the new Minister of Defence,' said Paul, re-enforcing Howard's revelation.

'Ok, my mistake. I mistook you for a crusty old pain in the arse who used to break into my house and steal my tea,' Danny said sarcastically.

'Mmm, that doesn't sound like me at all. Anyway, must go, Cabinet meetings and all that. We'll talk again soon, Paul,' said Howard, shaking Paul's hand before turning to Danny and extending his hand to him.

'Take care, Daniel, it's been a pleasure working with you,' he said, shaking his hand before walking out of the office.

'What the fuck just happened?' said Danny to Paul.

'A retirement of sorts, or a step towards retirement. None of us are getting any younger,' Paul said, noticing Danny still breathing a little heavily from running up the stairs.

'Yeah, yeah, I know, none of us are getting any younger,' Danny said, noting the look on Paul's face as he left his office.

His mobile rang as he settled down in his own office and trawled through the unread emails. Scott Miller's caller ID put a smile on his face as he answered.

'Scotty boy, glad you could pull yourself away from the keyboard to call me,' he said with a chuckle.

'Very funny, you caveman, glad you could pull yourself away from killing somebody to answer.'

'Ok, ok, what's up buddy?'

'I've been sent an invitation to a swanky new restaurant up west and thought, after recent events, you might like to join me and a couple of lovely lady friends of mine for an evening out,' said Scott, waiting for the excuse from Danny why he couldn't.

'Sounds good, mate, what time?' Danny said, surprising Scott.

'Oh right, marvellous, I'll pick you up at eight.'

'Great, I'll see you then.'

The rest of the day went by quickly as he caught up with paperwork and emails, the normality coming as a welcome change after recent events. He clocked off at five, shouting his goodnights as he left and headed home. He'd showered and changed by seven and was having a beer to start the evening off when the phone rang.

'Scotty boy, what's up?'

'Er, slight change of plan, Danny. Football ran a bit late, er, do you mind coming to mine before we go out?' Scott asked, his voice anxious and references off whack.

'Ok, I'll see you at eight,' Danny said, grabbing his keys and rushing out the front door the second he'd hung up.

For one thing, Scott never called him Danny, and for another, he wouldn't be caught dead playing football. Firing up his twin turbocharged BMW M4, Danny floored it, snaking off down the road in the direction of central London.

CHAPTER 71

I nstead of buzzing up to Scott to let him into the underground parking of his luxury Thames-front apartment block, Danny parked a hundred metres down the road. He opened the boot and grabbed the tyre wrench from the toolkit by the spare wheel. Tucking it inside his jacket, he walked towards the entrance. The memory of being bundled into a riot van last time he was here turned uncomfortably over in his mind. Remembering Scott's neighbour's name, he tapped the apartment number and waited for Mr Chilvers' face to appear on the screen.

'Hello.'

'Hello, Mr Chilvers. It's Scott's friend, Danny. I don't suppose you could buzz me in? Scott's intercom seems to be on the blink,' Danny said, giving him his best casual smile.

'Er, ok, here you go,' he said, the lock buzzing in front of Danny.

'Thanks,' Danny replied, pushing the door open.

He looked at the lift and then at the stairs. Although

271

not wanting to run up to the seventh floor penthouse apartment, the confines and vulnerability of being caught in the small, exposed lift made him head up the stairs. When he reached the landing, he stood for a moment, calming his breathing before moving silently to Scott's apartment door. He placed his ear on the wooden surface. All was quiet, no music playing, which was customary when Scott was building himself up for a night out. Danny moved across the landing and knocked on Mr Chilvers' door.

'Oh, hello, er…' said Mr Chilvers with a puzzled look on his face.

'Hi, sorry to bother you again. You won't believe it, Scott's door's jammed now. Million-pound apartments, huh, it's bloody disgraceful. You don't mind if I hop over onto Scott's terrace and sort it out for him? Thanks, Mr Chilvers, you're a star,' Danny said, talking quickly as he pushed past and headed out onto his balcony.

'What? Er, ok, I suppose,' stammered Mr Chilvers, looking more confused than ever.

Outside, Danny hopped over the glass divide onto Scott's patio terrace with its hot tub, sun loungers and views of the Isle of Dogs skyscrapers. He slid the tyre iron out of his jacket and moved close to the wall until he was beside the patio doors to Scott's lounge. Crouching down, he moved across until one eye could see through the glass. He could see the back of the sofa and the back of Scott's floppy, sandy coloured hair as he sat between a long-haired brunette and a blonde. Even from his view of their backs, Danny could see something was wrong. They were sitting bolt upright, facing forward, unmoving. Pulling his mobile out, Danny called Scott's number. He could see Scott's head move as he talked to somebody. The phone kept ringing until the imposing figure of Karl rose from the far side of the room, holding Scott's phone with one hand and a silenced handgun to Scott's head with the other. Keeping as low and tight to the wall as possible, Danny watched with one eye around the door frame as Karl held the phone on speaker in front of Scott.

'Er, hi, Danny,' he said in a bad imitation of keeping it cool.

'Hi, mate, your neighbour let me in. I'm at the front door,' Danny said, seeing Karl's head turn toward the apartment door.

Karl cut the phone dead before Scott could yell out to warn him. Turning his back to them, he headed off to the front door. As soon as he'd moved out of sight, Danny tried the handle on the patio doors, thankful to find them unlocked. He pulled them open and slid inside. With their hands and feet tied tightly together, Scott and the women jumped when Danny appeared in front of them with his finger to his lips. Leaving them, Danny followed the sound of metallic pings coming from the hall as Karl put four bullets through the apartment door. He yanked it open a second later, expecting to see a bullet-ridden Danny laying on the other side. When he was confronted with the empty landing, the penny dropped, and he spun around quickly.

Danny was already swinging the tyre iron as he turned, cracking it down on Karl's wrist, sending the gun clattering to the floor. Karl's face, still scarred and scabbed from the explosion at the Volkov mansion, contorted in a furious rage. He body tackled Danny, picking him up off his feet and charging him backward into the lounge, slamming him down onto the glass coffee table, the force shattering and bending it, leaving Danny lying in a pile of glass shards and bent metal legs. Winded and in pain, Danny swung the tyre iron wildly in front of him, catching Karl on the side of his knee as he grabbed Danny's throat with both hands.

Karl yelled in pain as he fell down on one knee, but his grip on Danny's throat only tightened.

'I kill you for my brother, for family honour,' Karl growled through gritted teeth.

Seeing stars and feeling close to blacking out, Danny stopped trying to hit Karl with the socket end of the tyre iron and thumped his fist down as hard as he could, sending the sharp end into Karl's thigh. As it split through his jeans and buried itself deep into his flesh until it hit bone. Yelling, Karl let go of Danny's throat and staggered to his feet. Gripping the tyre iron, he pulled it out of his leg. Gasping for air, Danny forced himself up and charged at Karl with every ounce of power he could muster, pushing him past the terrified women and Scott to crash out through the patio door in a shower of glass crystals. They tripped and fell awkwardly across the sun loungers, landing a couple of metres apart. Both men dragged themselves upright, breathing heavily as they stared each other in the eye.

The anger and emotion of the last few weeks boiled over. Danny's face set like granite, and his eyes darkened with murderous fury as he charged at Karl, ducking his swipes before launching a lightning combination of punches to the body and an uppercut to his chin. Karl staggered back onto the steel and glass railing at the edge of the terrace, his sky-blue eyes filled with hate as he reached inside his jacket and pulled a large hunting knife out.

'Family honour,' he growled.

'What's with you fucking lot and family honour?' Danny growled back, running forward to plant a flying kick to Karl's chest.

The blow pivoted Karl over the railing, his arms flailing helplessly as he tried and failed to get a grip on the railing before he fell out of sight. Picking himself up, Danny looked over the edge. Karl's body lay shattered by the entrance, blood pooling from beneath it as bystanders shrieked in shock. Turning away, he went back inside.

'Evening, Scott, ladies,' Danny said, untying them.

The women burst into tears, hugging each other in a mixture of emotions of fear, shock, and relief.

'I don't know whether to thank you or hit you, Daniel. Next time you want to invite one of your friends to the party, please don't,' Scott said, heading for the drinks cabinet.

'Well, I'd rather you didn't hit me, mate, I've had enough of that for one day,' said Danny, slumping down into the sofa.

'Mmm, yes, I suppose so. Here, you'd better have one of these,' said Scott, handing him a scotch.

'Thanks, so what time are we going out?' Danny said as all three of them turned to look at him.

ABOUT THE AUTHOR

Stephen Taylor was born in 1968 in Walthamstow, London.

I've always had a love of action thriller books, Lee Child's Jack Reacher and Vince Flynn's Mitch Rapp and Tom Wood's Victor. I also love action movies, Die Hard, Daniel Craig's Bond and Jason Statham in The Transporter and don't get me started on Guy Richie's Lock Stock or Snatch. The harder and faster the action the better, with a bit of humour thrown in to move it along.

The Danny Pearson series can be read in any order. Fans of Lee Child's Jack Reacher or Vince Flynn's Mitch Rapp and Clive Cussler or Mark Dawson novels will find these book infinitely more fun. If your expecting a Dan Brown or Ian Rankin you'll probably hate them.

Lightning Source UK Ltd.
Milton Keynes UK
UKHW042043020123
414704UK00004B/89